Reflections

A Modest Collection of Short Stories

by Sunny Franson

ISBN: 978-0-9855109-8-5 (Paperback, 2016)

Dedicated to Good Friends,
who have listened and offered
suggestions.

TABLE OF CONTENTS

Natural Energy

He walked along the dirt road in long strides because he was very tall, kicking up dust clouds with worn boots that had laces with numerous knots in them, where he had fixed them when they'd broken. His last ride, a trucker, had let him off at an intersection about half a mile back. The trucker was headed toward an interstate, and he didn't want to go in that direction.

Most of all he was thirsty, but he was hungry too and spotted a small group of stunted oaks about a quarter of a mile down the road. Otherwise there was only an occasional small tree here and there in the landscape, sometimes two trees. Dried grass and star thistle covered bare, hard soil that backed up to a few low, rolling hills that shimmered in the midday heat.

He knew he had to find something to drink and strode on toward the clump of trees, noting some low buildings with rusted metal roofs, clustered in and around the trees.

As he drew closer, he felt a heavy stillness in the air. Nothing moved, not even tall stalks of dried grasses and weeds. He wondered who would live way out here and why. There were no power lines going to the buildings and no vehicles parked around them, not even a bike, and no evidence of transportation of any kind.

He had a sinking feeling that the buildings were abandoned and there would be no water or food to be found here, but the closer he came, the more he thought that they didn't look so abandoned, because although the roofs were rusted metal, they were straight and tacked down. The sides of the buildings looked like they were made of some kind of composite material, but no parts of them looked to be sagging or out of square, like you'd expect to see with abandoned buildings. The whole place seemed vaguely like a contradiction in terms.

He walked over to the largest building. The front of it was mostly windows that extended down to about two feet above the foundation. Frames and sashes were straight and well positioned with no loose trim but were curiously weathered with flaking paint. There was no broken glass in the windows, and the lower halves were sparkling clean, but the upper halves appeared smudged and grimy. Faded curtains were hanging over each window, and bright flowers in colorful vases sat on each table by the windows. A washed out sign that said "Café" hung over the entrance.

He went to the front door, unsure of entering, but he was thirsty and hungry and at least needed water. He went inside.

At first the shelter away from the sun outside felt wonderful, but he also had trouble seeing around the room in which he found himself. It seemed so dark inside. His eyes quickly adjusted to the absence of the sun's glare, and he looked around to find someone to ask for water.

As he surveyed the room, he saw that it was long and narrow with tables and chairs lining the windows in front and a counter with stools drawn up to it running the entire length of the back wall. Behind the counter, along the back wall, was a cooking area including grill, stove top, oven and microwave. There was a pair of older refrigerators in one corner. Coffee pots, silverware, napkins and condiments were neatly arranged on the countertop behind which there was a workspace that ran the length of the counter. The place looked like a café straight out of the 1950's. He remembered the lack of power lines and figured they must have a generator.

As he blinked and looked around, he thought he spotted fleeting movement in one back corner. He blinked again and noticed someone quietly standing behind the counter toward the middle of the room. This was the only person he saw, so he walked over to the counter and said, "Do you think you could spare a glass of water?"

The woman behind the counter said, "Sure. How about some ice cubes in it?"

"Thanks," he said, "that would be great."

She got a glass from somewhere behind the counter, he heard clinking sounds, he heard water running, and she handed him a tall glass of water with several ice cubes in it.

"Thanks," he said. "I was hoping there'd be someone here. The place looked pretty quiet from the outside."

He drank most of the water, set the glass down, and she refilled it for him.

"Not really," she said. "There's always someone here," she added in a matter-of-fact manner.

As he looked over at her, he realized that she didn't seem to be much past her teens. She was slender with long, dark hair pulled back with a clasp, her eyes were large, dark and expressive but he couldn't tell what color they were, and her voice was quiet and melodious though tired. She had on a light blue uniform that did nothing for her, he thought, and she wore a white apron over it.

"You hungry?" she asked.

"Sure am," he replied. "I haven't eaten since early this morning. What do you have that's good?"

"Lunch special," she said, "Soup and sandwich. Potato soup and ham sandwich. If you want you can have some fruit and the sandwich."

"Thanks, I'll take the soup. It sounds good with the ham sandwich."

He sat down at the counter and was a little surprised, since the place was so quiet, when she ladled out a large bowl of steaming hot, thick potato soup and set the bowl and some silverware in front of him. Then she brought out some fresh bread and made a large sandwich with thick slices of what looked like honey baked ham, fresh lettuce, mayonnaise and mustard. She sliced it diagonally, put it on a plate and set it beside the soup. Then she began to wash glasses.

"Where you headed?" she asked conversationally.

"Nowhere in particular," he answered. "Just thought I'd

enjoy traveling around for a little."

"Not running from anything?" She chuckled.

"No, nothing like that. I just needed some time, that's all," he said.

"Sounds nice," she said, glancing over at him.

He felt obliged to say a little more. "I lost my wife some months back and wanted to be on the move for awhile and sort things out."

"Sorry to hear that." She spoke gently. "Your family must want to know how you are."

"No family," he spoke quietly, almost to himself. He had been eating hungrily and was beginning to slow down, and he was feeling tired now.

"Oh, sorry, I didn't mean to pry, " she said.

"Just need a little time to myself, I guess. Feels better to be on the road," he said. "And that sandwich sure hit the spot. A lunch like that keeps you going."

"Thanks." She nodded toward an oven that was beneath the stove top." "We like to bake the ham ourselves."

He peered at her. "How'd you come to be in a place like this?"

She was quiet for a moment.

"My turn to be sorry," he said. "It's none of my business."

"It's ok", she said. "A couple of years ago, I was traveling past, on my way to the interstate nearby, during semester break. My car broke down. Seems I just stayed on."

"Ever thought about leaving and going back to school?"

"Oh sure, but I just don't seem to have the energy for it any more," she replied. "Oh well, it's a nice, quiet life after all. No one comes by much, but that's fine. Nice and peaceful."

"Peace and quiet is nice. I wouldn't mind it for a while. I sort of need to figure out some things. You don't know of any place around here where I could stay just to take a little time for a few days or so, do you?"

"Well, if you want, there are a couple of rooms in two of those buildings over there." She pointed to two small, low buildings maybe a few hundred feet away, near some trees. "Twenty-five dollars a night."

"Guess I want to be somewhere with air conditioning," he said. "With maybe a few things to do, if I want."

"There's air conditioning. We have natural power. And you can eat here. Food's good and it doesn't cost too much. Only thing is it gets quiet around sundown. Just want to let you know that."

"So you have a generator?" he asked.

"Something like that," she murmured. "By the way, my name's Katherine, but most folks call me Katie."

"I'm Brian," he said. He was nearly finished with his lunch by now.

Brian thought about staying, but he didn't give much thought to the place itself. He was exhausted physically and emotionally, and all he really wanted was to be still and to rest before he moved on, if not here, then somewhere not too far ahead. But he was here already, where it was obviously quiet and where there was good food. He was tired with the kind of numb feeling that comes with stress and sorrow. He decided to stay overnight, anyway. He'd get an afternoon's rest, spend a quiet night, and leave in the morning.

"Ok," he said. "I'll take a room for the night."

He pulled out his wallet and paid for lunch and the room. Katie gave him a key, pointed to a building, and told him it was the room on the right. He thanked her, picked up his knapsack, and made his way out of the café and across the open yard to the room.

When he unlocked the door, he found a spare but clean and tidy room, with curtains that didn't quite fit over the lower windows. He really didn't care about the room. He turned on the air conditioner to cool the heat that had become trapped in the room. He was exhausted and fell asleep almost as soon as he stretched out on the bed.

When he awoke the afternoon had faded, and the outside temperature seemed to have dropped, if only a few degrees. That stifling feeling was still there, but he had the impression that it wasn't related to the heat of the day although he couldn't quite put his finger on why that was. He felt groggy from sleep and decided a shower and clean clothes would help.

When he emerged from his shower about twenty minutes later, his head still seemed to feel a little fuzzy even though he felt better overall. It was time for something to eat, he thought, and he remembered that Katie had mentioned that the place became very quiet after dusk. Outside there was no sound or movement anywhere in the immediate vicinity. He headed out the door and made his way to the café.

As he walked outside, he realized that he hadn't even heard any birds or insects, not earlier and not now either. That was odd, because insects usually began to emerge toward the end of the day if they hadn't been about in the hot sun, and birds were usually out to find food before nightfall when they went to roost. He had the impression that signs of life had faded.

Nothing had changed in the café. No one except Katie was there. She was standing in just about the same place as she had been earlier, almost as though she hadn't moved at all. He walked toward the counter and sat down on a stool.

"Hi," she said. "Did you get some rest? You looked completely exhausted earlier."

"Thanks," said Brian. "Yes, I do feel a little more rested, although I can't shake a feeling of being a little dazed or something. Maybe I was out in the heat for too long today. I'm already looking forward to a good night's sleep. And you were right about how quiet it is here. I didn't hear anything at all."

He looked more closely at Katie. She seemed to be more alert, and her eyes were bright and wide open. She seemed to have more energy than earlier in the day. He supposed that as the day cooled off, she felt better. He knew that he did.

He settled himself more comfortably on the counter stool and asked Katie what the dinner special was. She beamed and described the delicious meatloaf, thick homemade gravy and freshly mashed potatoes that were on today's menu. Fresh garden salad and creamy homemade thousand island dressing, fresh baked tiny sourdough loaves and good creamery butter went with the meal. She said that she made the meatloaf with chopped onion and garlic sautéed in a light white wine, and she roasted vegetables in a large, flat roasting pan until they were past tender and had broken down, so she could use the savory result to make a rue for the gravy, for which she used fresh, whole milk.

Brian couldn't believe his good fortune. Who would have imagined that this place would have food like that, he thought. Dinner would keep him going for quite a while. He was beginning to noticeably perk up. He was already feeling hungry and was delighted to see Katie pick up a large oval plate and head to the oven.

She opened the oven door and pulled out a huge, rounded meatloaf, seared and crisp on the outside, and sitting in golden gravy. She used a large metal spatula to slice off an entire end of the loaf and place it on the plate. From a saucepan on the stove she heaped a mound of mashed potatoes on the plate beside the meatloaf, she ladled gravy over all of it, spooned a large serving of buttered peas on the side of the plate, and set the food on the counter in front of Brian. To this she added a smaller plate of fresh, crisp green salad topped with the creamy dressing and croutons and another dish with two small, warm sourdough loaves along with a couple of heaping tablespoons of fresh, golden speckled butter.

Brian sighed happily. He breathed deeply, savoring the

delectable aroma that hung in the air around him and that rose in the steam from his dinner. It was quiet, he was hungry, there was good food in front of him, and life seemed to relax for a heartbeat.

"Thanks, thanks for everything, Katie," he said. "Say, have you eaten?"

"Not yet," she said.

"Why not fix a plate for yourself and join me? There isn't anyone else here right now, company would be nice, and you do need to eat."

She giggled a little and helping herself to a plate, she headed to the oven and stove where she prepared smaller portions of the same food. She pulled a stool around the edge of the corner from Brian, arranged silverware and a napkin and perched herself on the stool.

They ate in silence for a while. Then Brian asked, "What do you do for fun around here? Listen to the crickets, look at the stars, take walks?"

She looked just a little wary, he thought. She didn't say anything at first, continuing to eat but more slowly.

Then she looked over at him and shrugging her shoulders, replied, "There really isn't much to do here. Like I said, everything winds down about dusk. Here, let me get more bread."

She went part way down the counter and brought back two more small sourdough loaves and butter for them. She sat down on the stool again and took a loaf.

"At night you can see lots of stars around here," she finally said. "Skies are generally clear, but you have to hike over to that first small hill and climb it. Then you can see the whole sky. It just glows."

"Maybe I'll walk out that way then," he said. "Want to come along?"

"Oh, no thanks" she said. "I have too much to do after dinner."

He thought that probably wasn't true but said nothing. He was still very much wrapped in his own feelings. He'd just thought he was being social. When he thought about it, he realized that he hadn't been social for some months and had almost forgotten how.

He asked Katie if he could help her clean up, since no one else was there and it was growing dark outside now. He thought he'd help and then take that walk over to the low hill and climb it, enjoying the night air and the sky. If he got there in time he might even see what was left of the sunset.

Katie smiled cheerfully at him and thanked him for his offer but declined his help, suggesting that if he were going on his walk, he'd better go. After all, she said, he still looked tired and after the large meal, he might be drowsy.

As she began to clear the dishes, he thanked her for a great dinner, left money on the counter, wished her good night and walked outside. He walked slowly across the open yard toward his room but made his way around the building, heading for the small hill. It was too dark to see dust rise where he had walked, but he knew the dust was there. He could smell it.

Funny, he thought to himself, that he could smell the dust around here, but he hadn't seen or heard birds, and he didn't hear crickets. The absence of sound was loud. His senses felt almost prickly because some of them weren't being used.

The walk to the top of the hill didn't take long at all, and there they were, glistening and glinting in the night sky, stars by the millions or trillions, and constellations stretching far away, across the heavens. He recognized the Big and Little Dippers, Orion's Belt, Ursa Major, and a few others, but he didn't know that many of them. He wished he knew more and vowed to himself that in the future he would take time to enjoy the night sky and to learn more about it.

As he gazed at the horizons while slowly turning around, he didn't see any color to the west. The sun was well and truly gone for the day. He sat down and breathed in the night air.

He simply breathed. Then he realized that he had just had a fleeting thought about something he wanted to do in the future. For what seemed like a very long time he hadn't considered the future in any way that was not completely practical, like when he should do his laundry for instance, pay the phone bill, or water the lawn. Maybe the concept of a future was coming back into his life.

He stood there for fifteen minutes or so, completely relaxed, and then he began to make his way back to the enclave of buildings and to his room. Katie was right. He was feeling drowsy, and he also felt the beginning of giving in to the feeling of loss and grief, but in a sweet and sad way. It felt a little like he might have turned a corner of some kind.

When he reached the bottom of the hill, he could still easily find his way in the starlight. When he was fairly close to the grouping of trees and buildings, the air seemed to become thicker, and he felt as though he were almost swimming through it rather than walking. It seemed darker too. It was then that he thought to himself that his senses and feelings had been much sharper on the hill than they were here. He didn't especially care for that but by now he was sleepy and wanted to go on to bed. He made his way to his room by starlight that seemed to be fading too.

There were no lights in any of the buildings, except for the café. A small light glowed softly through a few windows. It looked like it was in the back, and it was not coming from the ceiling, shining down, but instead seemed to be coming from just below the height of the windows and was shining up. That was odd, but he was really quite tired, didn't want to investigate, and headed to his room. Only a few minutes later, he was drifting into slumber.

Suddenly he sat up straight, heart pounding and chest heaving. Why? What happened?

He looked out through the bottom of the windows. It was pitch black outside and there was no sound. No stars shone in the sky. Every nerve in his body was tingling, but he didn't understand why.

Then, there was a huge muffled sound like an enormous

implosion somewhere very close, and light was everywhere. It was bright white light, almost glowing and phosphorescent, and it illuminated all the buildings, trees, and nearby hills with its power. It was so strong it lit up building interiors, so that Brian's room was full of white light. It was so intense, it actually pulsed, ba-boom, ba-boom, ba-boom. Brian jumped up.

Then just as suddenly the light was gone, and complete darkness enveloped every corner and outside as well. Brian was wide awake and very alert. He quickly dressed and opened the door, peering around outside.

Silence. Nothing stirred, and there were no indications of life anywhere. He could barely see that dim light coming from the café, because the rest of the area was covered by what seemed like a thick, black fog. The darkness was so intense, he thought he could reach out and touch it.

He walked carefully and quietly toward the café, and when he got to within ten feet of the front door, he crouched and moved over to a window. He wanted to look inside but didn't want anyone to see him. He was still alert and wary.

He focused on the dim glow toward the back of the café and saw a small light that was about half way up the back wall and behind the counter. Katie was there. He thought he saw other movement, or had the impression of movement that was just below and behind the counter. All he could see was what might have been the top of something, less than an inch of it, and its owner seemed to be scurrying back and forth behind the counter.

Katie sat in front of the counter, on a stool near the back corner. She was in full view, and her head and shoulders were in silhouette from the soft light on the wall behind her. She was wearing what appeared to be a small cap made of a large mesh of some kind. Wires came from several places on it, running over the top of the counter apparently to something behind it, toward the floor.

When they were eating dinner, Katie had appeared vibrant, with luminous eyes, but now she looked completely exhausted. She had to brace herself with her hands. As she was doing that, she was staring at the wall sconce that Brian now noticed seemed to be almost throbbing, first softer, then a bit brighter. The pulsing didn't seem to follow a pattern of any kind, but it didn't seem to be random, either. Katie was staring at it, unblinking. She almost looked like she was in a trance. Brian looked carefully at the light but couldn't seem to figure it out, and for a moment there he wasn't sure of what he was seeing.

After what seemed like about twenty minutes, the light began to fade, and as it was slowly vanishing, Katie mechanically reached up and pulled off the small cap. It was pulled by its wires toward a spot out of sight behind the counter.

Katie stood up and began to make her way to the front door. Brian crouched down and backed up against the outer wall, making himself as invisible as he could. Illumination from the little light was nearly gone, but as Katie opened the door and went through it, she was again in profile from its very low light and from clean, clear, bright starlight now appearing overhead. He stared and had to force himself not to gasp. She looked horrible. He couldn't see her color in this light but she looked washed out, and the circles under her eyes were huge and black.

An owl called softly, and he saw its pale form as it silently flew over the clearing. He heard crickets chirping from the myriads of shadows created by the starlit sky.

Katie walked heavily and turned toward a building across the open yard. Brian watched her go and then when he thought it was safe, he crept, stooping, back to his room.

He didn't know how long he'd slept but was surprised that he'd slept at all. However the sun was already up when he awoke the next morning. He'd planned to make an early start and continue on his way.

Several weeks had passed, because around the clearing the stunted oaks were beginning to change color and the ground had a reddish grey tinge to it from angled sunlight. She made her way over the open yard, across the hard ground, to the long, low building with the faded sign that said "Café" over the entrance. She was irritable, because her car was a rental and it shouldn't have broken down. When she went inside, she blinked and after a few moments made out a tall male figure standing behind the counter, toward the middle. She asked for a phone because her cell wasn't working out here.

Expectations

If one were to ask a local citizen, "Do you know Thaddeus, Thaddeus Moody?" one might hear, "Why, sure, of course." "Everybody does." "Why sure, he's a good ol' boy." "Yep, the Moodys've been around just about as long as this town has." "Certainly, a real upstanding citizen of our community." "Oh, that dandy. Has a pretty good life here, his bein' a big wheel an' all in a little place like this." "Nice man, nice family. What's that you say? Well-liked – oh, is he well-liked? Oh, well, sure, I guess everybody's got a few enemies. Nobody's perfect you know."

Maybe the most suggestive reply would come from old Mr. Mayberry, a wizened, wrinkled gentleman with oddly shadowless grey eyes, who took his ease of afternoons in an old wicker chair in front of the general hardware store.

"Thaddeus Moody, eh? Well, you know any small town has a lot of surface talk and undercurrents. Well, people come packaged that way, too. It comes to my mind that Thaddeus does his share of visitin' around, bein' on committees, and bein' a general good guy, like any good citizen. But he's got his share of secrets. Oh yes, I think he does, that. You'll never see 'em though, at least not as they really are. If anyone ever talks about Thaddeus in a way he shouldn't have, you know, Thaddeus is the sort of person who'll come out ahead, no matter what, if he can."

When Thaddeus Moody passed the general hardware store each noon on his way to lunch at the corner lunch counter, he would incline his head, after a cursory fashion, in the general direction of old Mr. Mayberry. He felt slightly irritated at being obliged to follow the town custom of always greeting Mr. Mayberry. The firm, starched, narrow ellipse of a mouth, yellowing teeth, the eyes gazing vaguely downward from the heights of a medium to short, stocky frame, a scant widening of the nostrils, stubby, immaculately manicured nails on stocky fingers, on restless hands, the hint of a set, aggressive stride: none of this was lost on Mr. Mayberry, who saw the inherent contradictions in the carefully styled appearance and underlying motives of the personality projecting them. Mr. Mayberry recognized the need for a presence that would not normally be questioned because it suggested delineated boundaries. He'd always figured there were reasons for that but didn't spend any time thinking about it.

Thaddeus Moody, on the other hand, did spend time thinking about it and somewhat consciously collected himself into a personage that automatically remained at an unspoken arm's length from anyone's questioning him, his character, his life style, and his life. Oh yes, Mr. Mayberry was right. Thaddeus Moody did have secrets.

He paid somewhat conscious attention to his image, too. He was by nature rather self-absorbed and felt a general sense of entitlement. At times he actually lifted his nose and looked down it when in conversation with someone else, slightly tipping his head further and further back and therefore lifting his nose more and more when people were taller than he was. Unless you were looking for it, you didn't notice it, but you sensed it. Indeed, Thaddeus Moody did make his presence known.

He led an acceptably charmed life, by most standards. He had enjoyed a favored childhood, had gone away to a prestigious college where he had indulged in cloistered, protected, and boisterous fraternity life, he had returned to his family's quite successful, albeit small, town law firm, and he had continued to enjoy its rewards as he had helped to maintain its affluence and prestige. He was not really a Golden Boy but he was definitely a proprietor of the hierarchy sustained through generations in the small town. He and his family were members of admired social clubs and participated in admirably acceptable activities. He attended local men's clubs, as his father had done before him, as his brother and cousins did, and as the heads of households that were in the same social strata as his household did. Yes, Thaddeus himself felt his life was indeed a charming life.

Living always has its share of ups and downs, of open doors, of brick walls, and of potholes, along with lovely, cloistered, winding pathways from one point in time to another. This is true for everyone. It was true for Thaddeus Moody.

During his young manhood, he met a vivacious young lady named Margaret who was an altogether wonderful person but whose background was not quite as upstanding as many folks figured ought to be associated with someone like Thaddeus

Moody. Her single mother had been a woman of ill repute. Her father's identity was uncertain. Her own free spirit had been her means of pulling herself up by her proverbial bootstraps through her life and into college, where she met Thaddeus. Thaddeus was completely enamored, and he sincerely respected her for who she was. He fell deeply in love. She was an honest person who believed in him, trusted him, and remained true to him.

When he brought her to meet his family, they were pleasantly reserved, his father having already quietly investigated her and her family. Suffice it to say, Margaret's own accomplishments appeared to be not enough for them, and her happy demeanor grew quieter and ever more subdued. Within a week she left, because she, who was more worldly than Thaddeus, understood that some hurdles were better off left untried. Thaddeus was heartbroken and entertained plans of a future with her and without his own family, but she saw the potential for catastrophe, she was not quite as much in love with him as he with her, and she ended their relationship.

Meanwhile, before they went their separate ways, romance blossomed and Margaret became pregnant, but she did not know this until after she had met Thaddeus' family. She never did tell Thaddeus whom she saw only once after that visit. That was when she told him their relationship was over.

Although Thaddeus never knew then about the pregnancy and he never saw Margaret again, a few years later during a chance encounter and subsequent luncheon with college chums, he learned that Margaret had passed away, it seemed during a difficult childbirth. The baby had not survived.

No one knew who had been the father, and Thaddeus didn't suspect that it might have been himself. Reference to Margaret had been brief, conversational, and without any reference or details that might have given rise to suspicions about his having been the father, but still he entertained what was in his mind pure fantasy of his having fathered a child with his beloved. It never occurred to him that it might be true, and it made him happy to dream.

Thaddeus was not complex that way.

Over time, and once again back home, he joined the family law firm and began to handle more and more of the estate business, and he squired a few of the generally appropriate single women in town to local dinners, dances, law firm parties, and even county fairs. He was in no way a man about town at least as far as the ladies were concerned. However, he was learning more and more about who owned what in the small community, and he enjoyed an acceptable process of finding a wife.

After a few years he did find one. They married, bought a nice, older home on a quiet street lined with large, mature, comforting trees, under whose shade were mothers walking with strollers, children riding bikes for newspaper routes, and nearby, a couple of fishing holes in a fairly good sized creek that meandered through that part of town.

After a few more years, they started a family, and finally after a few more years elapsed, had two daughters and one son, each a few years apart. Their son was the oldest of the three.

Thus began times with Boy Scouts and Girl Scouts, music lessons and Little League, ballet lessons and school programs, and eventually baseball, soccer, and football. Their children were active and outgoing in general, although they had assimilated their father's demeanor of being a trifle reserved and observant of other people, who they were, how they behaved, and what their standing in town was, along with the inference of what it might be that they had.

The children didn't realize they were absorbing this kind of knowledge or what might be done with it. They simply mimicked their father. Their lives were still open books with a horizon full of directions from which they could choose.

Thaddeus Moody's life was everything it had been expected to be, by his parents' standards. Although he didn't realize it, Thaddeus himself had paid a price for having followed in the footsteps his family had established over a few generations. He didn't know that he might have wanted something else out of life. The part of him that had been so deeply drawn to Margaret had never blossomed or spread out further, so he didn't know what it was.

Still, those potentialities, even though unrecognized, were small, unfulfilled dissonances within his persona and by being squelched, had morphed over time into a sort of cynicism. This seemed to emerge at times in connection with his business of being a lawyer. Since he was knowledgeable about people and their belongings, their trials and tribulations, deeds, possessions, inheritances, final wishes, waiting family members, financial arrangements, and more, he was in a position to know when someone needed a favor, or a loan, or something else. He did not ever take illegal advantage, but he knew who could pay a full price for services rendered, who needed an extension on a mortgage, who might be open to an equitable trade, who might need a helping hand, and so on.

Because Thaddeus was a quiet sort and because he was shrewd enough to publicly show that side of himself, he was considered to be a repository of confidentialities of those who came to him for business. It was of course a given part of his business, and he allowed it to blossom.

Over time, his position in the business, social, and political side of the small town became ever more important although never in an obvious way. He was in a position to pull strings and to exert pressure if he chose to do so. As a rule, he didn't, although there had been a few occasions when "an equitable trade" situation had happened. Those were always kept transparent, with appropriate assessments and open records, and they worked well.

Thaddeus was truly growing into Mr. Mayberry's thoughts of him as a person about town. Even Thaddeus didn't realize everything meant by that, but he did thrive on continuing to be observant, careful, and fastidious in his habits, never incriminating himself in any way, and yet knowing more about many folks than was comfortable for them.

His profession had instilled a residual aggression within him. His nature was not normally expressive of aggression, but over the years, in defending his clients and in being observant so his impressive, private repository of hidden knowledge grew, he had picked up a certain blunt, unforgiving approach in some ways. He had actually begun to appreciate a sense of entitlement about himself.

He was aware that old Mr. Mayberry saw these things about him, and he didn't appreciate being emotionally, financially, spiritually, or in any other way visible to someone whom he did not place in a special position in his world, or in any way being transparent to anyone at all. He had built his world, it was nicely arranged, and he didn't want anyone else to be all that familiar with it. His family didn't know specifics of some parts of his life, and he liked it that way. His family was everything to him, but they existed in a different sphere.

So, he inwardly cringed a little when he saw laser like eyes returning his look when he said "Hello" to Mr. Mayberry as he passed by. Mr. Mayberry's obvious acuity regarding human nature gave him an uneasy feeling, although he had no idea why, because he hadn't really done anything wrong. He was annoyed that someone might see something, anything, about his life that he was used to keeping to himself.

The old adage that a rather silent and unapproachable way of doing things, such as business, always seemed to leave an aura of secrecy in its wake was relevant in his case. Secrecy seemed to invite clandestine operations that might occur in the small town, whatever those could possibly be. A lack of transparency always seemed to invite eyes that wanted to peek behind a curtain to see what was there. It didn't matter that nothing in particular was there.

Thaddeus Moody continued on his way to the corner lunch counter, went in, and seated himself at a corner booth where he could see most folks who walked by, but where they couldn't see him very well. Although he didn't actually spend much time simply watching people walk past, going about their business, he did like to be the one who did the noticing rather than the one whom people noticed. He ordered his usual, a ham sandwich on rye with potato salad and coffee, and settled in for a nice lunch. He was hungry.

When Dick Stegler came over to say Hello, he felt a little put out because he liked this time to himself. Dick Stegler owned the local hardware store and was a personable sort who enjoyed being friendly with his customers and who was generally already aware of what they might need.

"Hi there, Thaddeus," said Dick. Thaddeus replied in kind. Dick didn't sit down across from Thaddeus, in the booth.

"You busy this afternoon? I got somethin' I want to get your opinion about."

"Can you come by a little later, say, around four or so?"

"Sure, see you then," Dick said.

Thaddeus Moody gave a little wave as Dick turned and walked away. He turned back to his ham sandwich, potato salad, and coffee.

Yes, Thaddeus Moody was a quiet sort, thought Dick Stegler, but he liked that in a lawyer. He didn't notice what Mr. Mayberry saw, that Thaddeus Moody preferred to remain quiet because he preferred to gather in potential information rather than offer it. He scooped in instead of ladling out.

Dick had gone back to his store by the time Thaddeus finished his lunch, paid for it, left a tip, and got up to leave. He quietly and efficiently made his way past tables and chairs, some of them occupied and some of them empty, and headed out the door to return to his office and the appointments he had, plus paperwork he wanted to finish by the end of the day before Dick Stegler came by.

When Dick arrived later on, work was winding down and Thaddeus was ready for him. Thaddeus beckoned to the comfortable chair on the opposite side of his desk, and Dick sank into it and became subdued, although he couldn't seem to stop his fingers from slightly, continuously twirling about themselves. Thaddeus saw that he was nervous.

Finally he said, "I just found out I have a half brother."

Thaddeus regarded Dick intently and waited for him to go on.

"I haven't met him," Dick went on, "but we talked on the phone last night. He called me. He knew about me."

Thaddeus waited.

"I guess my dad was married before," Dick said. "We never knew. When Dad died last year, he left a letter with the attorney who passed it along."

He went on, "Dad told him about my sister and me. He told him how to reach us and left it up to him to decide if he wanted to do that. I don't know why we never knew about him."

"I guess we'll find out why, because he wants to meet us. He's coming to visit this weekend." Dick took a deep breath.

"I don't know how I'm going to handle it. I guess it'll depend on who he is as a person."

He stopped for a few minutes, then said, "I'm nervous. I'm not sure what he's expecting from us. I'm looking forward to meeting him though."

Thaddeus said, "Well, Dick, what a surprise. Out of the blue. You didn't have any sense of this before?"

"No", Dick replied.

"What can I do for you?" Thaddeus asked.

"Well, we don't know if we need to do anything, you know, with paperwork. Dad left the hardware store to me. I've been running it anyway since he retired."

"As you know, after Mom died a few years ago, he decided to leave the estate to Bev and me. I know there wasn't a lot, but the store is what I do for a living, and my family needs it. I just don't know what this guy wants." Dick didn't think of him as a brother yet. It was too new.

"You know, I want to meet the guy and get to know him. I want to welcome him. He's my half brother, but I'm not sure what he wants. Do you think there might be something we need to do before he gets here?"

Dick meant something that would be legal and binding. It was a delicate moment. Clearly, he wanted to believe that everything about this would be positive and good, but his protective instincts said, Caution.

Thaddeus folded his hands together on his desk. "Your father's wishes were legally recorded, and they were specific, so I don't think you need to worry. There aren't any loopholes there."

He paused. "What would concern me is that someone who has ulterior motives might try to gain your trust and use that as a way to manipulate you or your sister. You're wondering if there is a reason for you to protect yourself, so in a way, you're already alert about meeting this man. You know, it never hurts to be careful and take things a step at a time."

Those words of advice more or less summed up how Thaddeus Moody approached life. He was paid to be who he was. He lived in the best of both worlds. What he also did was subtly impair spontaneity and joy that Dick might have experienced when he welcomed a new member into the family.

Dick thanked Thaddeus and said goodbye. "Good evenin' to you, and thanks. I guess I'm feeling a little relieved now. If anything comes up, you know what's going on, and let me know if anything occurs to you. Regards to the family."

Thaddeus thanked him, also sending good wishes along, and Dick Stegler left the office.

Thaddeus placed his hands on his desk again, fingers steepling. Something about this didn't set well with him. He wished he knew more about Dick Stegler's father's first marriage, and why the family that he had raised in this small town wasn't aware of a past. Perhaps there was sorrow, anger, or something else involved, or perhaps something unseemly was involved.

Thaddeus almost unconsciously made a point to himself to offhandedly, discreetly be particularly attentive to small talk about town. Truthfully, this was what Thaddeus Moody did anyway, without thinking about it at all. In a way, he was an unbidden proprietor of the little town's morally honest life and also its less than appealing, seamier life.

It didn't matter on what side of town a person set up housekeeping or in which social circle a person interacted with others. Less than appealing sorts of things were found across the board, and Thaddeus had come across most of them.

Unfortunately, many people recognized that about him. Some admired him for his astute but never divulged knowledge, some were ill prepared to trust or respect him, some were less than comfortable in his presence, but nearly everyone unconsciously saw him as a potential threat.

Thaddeus was not so naïve that he was unaware of this effect. Since he was by nature someone who was not open with his thoughts, feelings, and conclusions, and since that felt entirely natural to him, he did not realize that this secretive demeanor might be the source, or at least one of them, of extreme feelings people might have about him.

He thought that most folks generally kept up with their own sensibilities, but he didn't take into account that some folks might be driven by various dreams, wishes, nightmares, or imagined or real stressful situations, and were in some way already cornered within their own lives. Thaddeus didn't realize that even a tiny threat could be the catalyst that would topple someone's hold on control or sanity.

He couldn't realize that, because his way of being in the small town was simply an extension of who he was, and due to his attachment to the way he felt "things should be", his imagination didn't wander too far on either side of his own behavioral fulcrum. He was always astonished when someone did something outrageous, even when others were not surprised at all.

For instance, if someone were hiding something away and someone else knew of it, and that someone else were to use it as leverage in one way or another and hired Thaddeus to apply some leverage so it would be done legally, the first someone might assume that Thaddeus would have been told whatever it was that was being hidden away.

Since Thaddeus was so observant, he probably would know, but even if he didn't and someone were angry and cornered, Thaddeus himself might unknowingly become a target.

Such was vaguely the case with Dick Stegler and his previously unknown half brother. Dick was not an unkind person. He didn't believe in creating barriers where they weren't needed. There had been something in the man's voice when he'd called Dick, explaining who he was and that he'd like to meet the rest of the family. He was friendly, and he was very curious about his deceased father's business rather than who he had been as a person and why he had never been a part of his first son's life. There were also questions about the hardware store.

His name was Frank Bonham. Frank wanted to know how large the store was, what it had, who ran it, and finally, who owned it. He was clearly interested in any possible inheritance. He'd always known that his mother received money from somewhere, not a lot but enough for them to get by. She had worked, and with both incomes, they had actually had a comfortable life. She had always told him that her first husband had left them high and dry, and that there was a small monthly income from her second husband, his father, who had died not long after their marriage had ended in divorce.

Frank had grown up without a father, he had been resentful at times, and he had often been a handful for his mother. He had begun drinking at fourteen. That habit had never gone although he wasn't technically an alcoholic even if he did depend on it sometimes to help him face his emotions. He was able to use enough control to maintain his employment.

His mother was gone now, and the small monthly income was passed on to him. What he didn't know was that this income was actually from an annuity his father had set up for him and his mother in lieu of alimony.

He had never heard good things about his father, because his mother was resentful that she had been asked for a divorce, not the other way around. The divorce was not friendly, mother and son had moved away, and she had not wanted any contact. An attorney had handled financial matters, and she had simply received a monthly stipend from the annuity.

Frank's formative years had included anger and judgment. He never knew why his parents had divorced but had guessed it was probably largely his father's fault. Through the years, he'd been referred to juvenile authorities a few times, and as an adult he'd been on probation for petty theft. Eventually he'd found work in a local foundry, had learned the trade, and had made his way into a position that allowed a decent income. He'd have liked to retire early, but that wasn't possible.

He didn't know the hardware business at all, but he dropped a few remarks to Dick, implying that he was familiar with it and would like to know more. Dick picked that up, and he didn't like it. He wanted to meet his half brother free of judgment but was wary because of subtle references to the hardware store. He didn't know what Frank's financial situation was, and Frank didn't know that the small stipend he received was what their father had established for him and his mother. There were many unknowns and too many conjectures.

The day came when Dick Stegler and his family met Frank Bonham and welcomed him into the family. People remained reserved to be sure, until they took full measure of one another. Dick remained uncomfortable with Frank's obvious interest in Dick's assets. Dick had worked hard for his parents, for his family, and for the small town as well.

After the large, extended family enjoyed grilled hamburgers and potato salad at the backyard picnic table, when

Frank mentioned he would enjoy visiting the hardware store, Dick let slip that he had seen his attorney in case there would be something he would need to do or adjust when he learned of the existence of a half brother. He was assured that everything was in order, and their father's wishes had been followed. Frank understood, but his face clouded over before he could hide his reaction.

Here was a difficult situation.

Frank didn't know that his stipend existed because his father had foresight enough to arrange alimony in a manner that would provide for his mother, and then for him. He figured that the attorney in question had executed a will that was in favor of his half brother Dick, and that he had been left out.

In his resentment, his imagination blossomed and he assumed that the attorney had probably known about him and had sided with friends. He imagined that the attorney had researched him and had learned about his past. Frank's mother had been a basically angry person, and he had learned how to live as an angry person himself.

Dick naturally didn't know about the stipend or how it had come about. He didn't know about Frank's mother and her volatile nature, and he fervently wanted the afternoon to be over. He didn't offer to visit the hardware store so Frank could see it, and he decided not to ask Frank back again. The next move would be up to Frank, friendly or otherwise. He hoped there would not be a next move.

Thaddeus Moody didn't know anything about any of it.

As an attorney he was certainly aware of human nature enough to understand that people can be opportunists, and sometimes seedy ones at that. It wasn't necessary for him to know details of what was happening between Dick Stegler and Frank Bonham. He only knew what was needed to do his job. He was a careful person.

None of this was enough to keep Thaddeus Moody from harm, especially if his own rather ordered way of life didn't allow him to foresee chaotic events. The unknowns in Dick Stegler's and Frank Bonham's recent connection were becoming chaotic.

After that afternoon, Dick Stegler felt unsettled and unsure about what he ought to do, as far as Frank was concerned. His reaction was wary, and he wasn't by nature a wary person. He was extremely uncomfortable, and he felt protective of his family. At the same time, he felt that the proper thing to do was to try to get along with his half brother. That's what family did. It was how his parents had raised him and how he had raised his own family. He didn't want to betray his beliefs in family bonds, but he was not a foolish man and realized that this situation was far from optimal.

On the other hand, Frank Bonham was something of a loose cannon because he was used to the strength that his constant, underlying anger gave him. When he left Dick's home that afternoon, he sensed that he was not actually welcome and that he was not going to be offered part of what his father had bequeathed. This left him frustrated, upset, and aggressive in a churlish way. He made his way back home and began to drink to dull the edgy feeling.

Their father had kept his past to himself because he had thought this was the best solution, once he had understood that he could never remain married to Frank's mother when he had seen how different their core values were, even though she was the mother of his child. The best he could do was what he had done. He had provided for her financially as best he could. When he met and married Dick's mother, whose beliefs either matched or complimented his own, his first wife had created several ugly scenes, and for the sake of their marriage, Dick's parents had distanced themselves from her and the very young child. They felt they had no choice.

Thus, secrets began. If only Frank's mother had been open with her son about his father and the annuity. If only Dick's parents had not felt the need to protect their family from his first wife. If only. In a perfect world there might never be a need for "if only's". In any other world, secrets have a way of being a source of ever expanding collateral damage.

Frank Bonham ate dinner alone. After dinner, he continued to drink, but he was able to work the next day, and the next, although as usual his anger and frustration were basically in charge of his life. He was watchful of his behavior when not at home, and he managed to get by.

On the third day after his visit, a letter came. It was from the attorney who handled the annuity. In the recession, it had lost some value, not much, but enough to slightly lower his monthly stipend. He understood the logic involved, and he knew that when the economy turned around, his monthly allotment would increase. But it was easier for him to be angry and to look for a reason for the way he thought his life had turned out.

He figured that the attorney Dick said he'd seen had probably orchestrated his being left out, or sold out, as he put it to himself.

The next day, he wasn't able to hold himself together at work. Many times over the years, he'd been asked to leave his bad attitude at home. This time, and because work had been slow for a long time, he was laid off. Nothing was fair.

The next day, he returned to see Dick Stegler but decided to go around to that attorney's office first. As he was ushered into Thaddeus' office, without an appointment, he pushed his way past Mary, the secretary, and came face to face with a rather prissy, carefully groomed, smallish man, not with the bullish, brash individual he expected Thaddeus to be.

Thaddeus Moody recognized that Frank Bonham was deeply upset and perhaps also deeply disturbed. He could smell alcohol. He didn't think more about that and introduced himself to Frank after Frank said who he was. Thaddeus figured that Frank might want to confirm that his and Dick Stegler's father had written a legal will and that he'd been left out of it.

"I'm glad you met Dick", said Thaddeus pleasantly.

"Who cares," said Frank.

"He isn't happy that I'm around," he added. "What about

heading into the hardware store? Maybe I can take some sort of action there."

Thaddeus Moody didn't care for the way Frank phrased that, but it wasn't his place to form an opinion, so he said, "What happens at the hardware store is up to Dick. It and everything about it belongs to him."

"Well, that's that," snorted Frank. "I'm out in the cold."

His voice went up a few notches. "What do they care?" I'm just a good for nothing half brother. They don't even have to recognize me if they don't want to."

He stood up and began pacing back and forth, punching the window curtains every time he passed them. His hands were balled into fists.

Then he said, "Why didn't you tell them that they needed to include me? Why did you tell them that everything was buttoned down tight so they didn't need to worry? Why did you?"

He kept pacing but stared over at Thaddeus as he paced.

"It isn't my place to tell my clients what to do," replied Thaddeus, who had begun to back away, increasing any open space between Frank and him.

This only served to infuriate Frank even more, he paced faster, and he swung out at the curtains and at Thaddeus' desk.

"All I want is a *break*," he shouted full out now. "I deserve a break. Ya know what, I'm gonna take it."

With that he turned and grabbed at the heavy crystal paperweight on the desk and threw it at the wall. Unfortunately,

Thaddeus was on his way to the door, wanting out. His left temple collided with a sharp corner of the paperweight full on, and he went down, out cold and bleeding.

Frank panicked and ran toward a side door to the street. He left without checking Thaddeus or calling for help.

It was bad luck that the paperweight's sharp corner nicked a fairly large blood vessel in Thaddeus Moody's temple, he bled profusely, and he died without ever coming back to consciousness.

It was more bad luck that Mary had gone out to collect some office mail that had been held at the post office for signatures. She wasn't at her desk in the outer office when Frank had raised his voice. She didn't find Thaddeus until she looked in to tell him she was going to lunch. She only did that because she hadn't seen him pass her desk on his way to his own lunch, and that was his usual custom.

In the ensuing investigation, Mary was able to describe Frank Bonham to the police fairly well. She had heard of his visit to town a few days earlier. Like many of the townsfolk, she had heard who he was, why he had suddenly appeared in town, what kind of clothes he wore, if he had decent manners, and considerably more. Many in the little community had heard everything, and what people didn't know, they invented by way of embellishment.

The town was buzzing. Old Mr. Mayberry didn't have to say anything. He simply listened, and he discerned what had happened but wasn't quite sure why. All he knew was that Thaddeus Moody didn't deserve to die, that his nature predisposed him to a certain amount of distrust from others, that something about that whole piece of it played into this, and that the Moody family was suffering a great loss, although Thaddeus would have been certain to have arranged that they would have ample income should something happen to him.

Mr. Mayberry understood that there were twists and turns that were a part of Thaddeus Moody's death. They just hadn't come to light yet. No matter. Frank Bonham ought never to have thrown a heavy object in a rage, in an office that belonged to someone he didn't know and who didn't know him.

Mr. Mayberry knew that these things happen, and he understood that it would likely be the sum of little things that had led up to the final outcome. He was curious about what those little things might be, but the truth was that he didn't give the matter too much thought. He sat back in his wicker chair, watched people coming and going, saw who needed something at the hardware store, watched people on their way to lunch, and said "Hello" or nodded his head to folks going by.

He understood the ways of the world. He understood that while Thaddeus Moody shouldn't have died, the manner in which he did die was not entirely accidental, even when anything to do with Frank Bonham's presence and temper was omitted.

Mr. Mayberry understood that the knowns and unknowns of the world swirled around in complex fractals, blending with the infinite variations of human nature. In Thaddeus Moody's case, the resulting ordered chaos might have happened at any time in his life, anywhere in his life. This time, the changes that were created actually took his life. Perhaps Thaddeus Moody had vaguely recognized what Mr. Mayberry understood and hadn't liked it, or Mr. Mayberry, very much.

Authorities had a very clear picture of what had happened at the law office. They had interviewed Mary, several townspeople, Dick Stegler, and were branching out into Frank Bonham's home town and background.

When they processed the crime scene, for they believed it was a crime scene, they found Frank's fingerprints and Thaddeus' blood on the paperweight. Since he had found himself on the wrong side of the law a few times when he was much younger, Frank's fingerprints were on file, although he hadn't been around anyone who had died before. This was duly noted.

They found Frank Bonham and heard what he had to say. When the coroner concluded his report, he more or less agreed with Frank's story.

Careful study of the head wound revealed rather precisely how Thaddeus had received the fatal blow and from which direction it had come. By and large, Thaddeus' death was accidental, an unexpected turn of events, a movement in the wrong direction at the wrong time.

Frank Bonham had not aimed the paperweight at Thaddeus, and he had not premeditated anything. But it was Frank's anger that was the catalyst to the temper tantrum that resulted in his throwing the paperweight that killed Thaddeus Moody.

Aside from never learning to control his negative approach to life or to keep his temper in check, Frank made the mistake of not immediately calling for help as well as not calling the authorities.

It was unlikely that Thaddeus could have been saved. He hemorrhaged from the wound into his own cranial cavity, and that happened within a few minutes. He died quickly from blood loss and suffocating pressure on the brain. It was unlikely that he would have recovered even if emergency personnel had been able to revive heartbeat and respiration.

However, Frank ran away from the scene of a life threatening accident, and there were legal consequences for that. He was questioned, was told to remain in town, and was watched carefully as authorities fleshed out details of the case and formulated proof for appropriate charges against him.

It was during this investigation that authorities located and spoke with the attorney who was in charge of the small annuity. They learned who had established it, how it had been used, and how it was now being used.

When they spoke with Dick Stegler, and then with Frank Bonham, about that, they learned that neither had known that their father had arranged it, the reason for it, and anything connected with it. Everyone involved learned more about facts, behaviors, and emotions surrounding their father's first marriage than had even been imagined.

News traveled fast as usual, and soon people understood that Thaddeus Moody did not know all the details himself, even if he was a secretive sort. Most were shocked, some were saddened, and others brought casseroles and baked goods to the Moody family's front door.

Old Mr. Mayberry sat unperturbed in the wicker chair in front of the hardware store. He was taking in all the latest news, but he, for one, was not surprised by it. He did feel badly for all the misfortune in general and hoped that the Moody family would recover. He knew that they would.

In time, after the funeral, the Moody family began to recover. The children returned to school, and Mrs. Moody began to attend a few small social events again. Local men's clubs honored their former member Thaddeus Moody and then went on with the business at hand. The few other lawyers in the Moody family law firm took care of Thaddeus' clients. It was not yet known if one or more of his children would entertain the law as a profession, but the business was on solid ground and would eventually need one or more attorneys as the current ones eventually cycled out into retirement.

At first, Dick Stegler was taken aback with the news that his father had taken care of his first family, although he felt good about that. Not only did he feel it had been the ethical and honorable thing to do, the knowledge surreptitiously enabled him to allow any guilt about not wanting to help Frank Bonham, and any anger toward his father for having brought this situation into his life, to fade away. He hadn't consciously been aware of guilt or anger, but now he felt an ease of mind that he didn't quite expect but for which he was grateful. A burden seemed to have been lifted from the inner workings of his consciousness.

On the other hand, Frank Bonham hadn't lost his general grudge against just about everything. He was too used to carrying it around and using it as a crutch. Life was easier that way. He wasn't generally challenged by it and if by some chance he were, he had an escape hatch.

In a way Frank felt robbed because he had never known a father, but the antagonistic approach he had learned by imitating his mother gave him a certain strength and allowed him an outlet for his usual anger whenever he needed it. Frank felt safer that way. He was used to allowing himself to fall prey to anger. It actually felt comfortable. He could remain angry at his father.

In a way, not much had changed. Dick Stegler had gone through a trying time but had emerged from it not unscathed, but all right.

Frank Bonham hadn't changed much either, although he was facing a future in which he would need to account for what had happened and would be responsible for dealing with any charges for which authorities had sufficient proof. At the very least, he ought not to have left the scene of an accident.

Thaddeus Moody had lost his life. This time, Thaddeus

Moody had not come out ahead.

His family and its future were forever altered, although perhaps not as much as might initially be presumed. Values, morals, social circles, peer pressures, individual personalities, boundaries within societies and even accepted beliefs that were prevalent in neighborhoods didn't change. Systems remained in place. People were held within those systems, sometimes at the centers, sometimes on the edges, but always buffered by their presence and constancy.

Spikes in this constancy came about with Thaddeus Moody's death, but the inherent order within such systems eventually absorbed them and leveled them out. Life went on.

Old Mr. Mayberry understood these ways, although detached as he was because he was an observer, he was inclined toward cynicism. Now and then he noticed children coming from school, walking down the main street of town. Once in a while, he saw one or more of the Moody children. They were following in their father's footsteps, he noticed. Yes, life went on. There would always be hiccups.

Mr. Mayberry wondered what it would take for an upheaval that would actually make a difference, upending some of the more entrenched social structures and furthering different approaches to how people lived.

He knew events like wars had done this, and enormous natural disasters did this as well, but even with these the changes didn't seem lasting. They might be established for years, maybe even a century or two, or more, but eventually the usual cycles seemed to emerge once again.

Prosperity, depression, harmony, disparity, abundance, drought, war, and peace fluctuated through time. When viewed from a distance, what seemed to be chaos didn't appear chaotic, only as threads that were as fluid and as separate and simultaneously intertwined as ripples from splashing raindrops on the surface of a pond in a woodland meadow during summer rain showers.

Old Mr. Mayberry sometimes mused about the possibilities for the balance of the range of possibilities of human nature to be situated more to the side of peace rather than war, or indeed, more to the side of war rather than peace. He didn't know. He didn't have answers. As an observer, he simply wondered.

It occurred to him that this balance existed in other ways too. He figured it measured what represented not only civilization but also groupings such as nations, and also features within individuals. Then it would be up to the individual to try to create balance toward the side of peace and harmony. He wondered if that were even possible.

Mr. Mayberry didn't wonder for very long. He was after all an observer of what happened beyond himself as an individual. He was content to simply relax in his wicker chair, saying "Hello" to friends, neighbors, and acquaintances, and remain the observer that he was. Whatever wisdom he had gained in his lifetime was more a matter of absorption than of analysis. He was wizened but not necessarily cerebral about it all.

Most of the people walking along the sidewalk nodded

to him as they walked by. A few didn't look didn't look directly at him, although those folks knew he was there and some were actually keenly aware of his presence. A few greeted him and shook his hand.

The little town collectively breathed deeply and settled itself into the dusty summer.

Mushroom

It was born when its parent shed spores in a powder puff cloud that dissipated in a gentle breeze, dispersing the cloud's contents in close proximity to the parent clump. It landed in a deer track pressed into moist forest humus, it swelled to at least ten times its dehydrated size, and it began to grow. At first it grew slowly as its cells needed time to reproduce and to mature but this process advanced exponentially, and then it grew very rapidly.

It felt comforted in the knowledge that other spores were evolving into adults close by, since conditions were very good and the parent had puffed out many potential children. As they grew, they began to realize that there was only so much room in the deer track, and they began to bend and curve to accommodate each other, reaching for more growing space.

This was not unusual. Eventually each became its own adult and sent out spores that colonized soft, moist earth up to a foot or so away. In this way each individual lived on, over and over and over again.

Most individuals seemed to end up in clumps of their own kind, and over time, the quiet forest became studded with individual mushroom clumps, each with close ties to generations of spores dating back to one spore. It was difficult to know which came first: the spore or the mushroom.

As space became less available and individual clumps began to encroach upon each other's area, some groups began to appear less robust than other groups.

It became apparent that there wasn't enough nutrition or attention to needs in an osmotically orchestrated habitat for each and every individual clump. Groups of clumps began to form and within these groups, individual clumps found their outlook toward existence changing, as they needed to adapt to less space, or to more aggressive clumps, or to clumps that seemed to be sedate but that nevertheless strove toward the best nutrition and light available in the neighborhood.

The original mushroom-turned-clump found itself in a state of observation and was not certain what the best way to exist would be. It simply existed and assumed that other clumps were doing the same, sharing life, and sharing space when necessary but needing to survive too. Each time one clump moved in a little on another clump, or the land went dry for a bit for lack of rain and fog, clumps retreated into spore mode and appeared again in more benevolent times.

The mushroom clump noticed that all the clumps had the facility to learn and to grow, and that each seemed to grow in a subtle but individual way. This was a good thing, as then all clumps would not be the same. However this mushroom clump was inherently a quiet clump and tended to grow and then fade, grow and then fade again, and to retreat into spores that floated a bit further away from clumps that seemed to need better soil or more moisture or that seemed to be more aggressive.

Eventually, the mushroom clump became a bit aged and wizened, which was good as it could adapt to change and loss, but not good as it had gradually grown apart from other clumps and seemed unable to compete with them in their space. Eventually, it preferred not to compete, adapting itself even more to a habitat that was not especially appealing to other clumps generations away from their original spore heritage, and moving itself further away from the main stream.

As time passed and clumps flourished and faded, flourished and faded, the mushroom clump seemed to venture toward other clumps now and then by means of stray spores. However these spores were now not the same as the original group of spores had been, way, way back in time. They seemed to be the same and some parts of them were the same, but other parts had grown in different ways. The closeness of the first set of spores was no more, and in fact there were undercutting maneuvers from some spores that saw new spores as a threat.

Fortunately the mushroom clump had evolved enough to keep to itself and to still survive, and to understand that the basis of all, and for all, was survival. It kept on existing, sending out spores, regenerating itself at times closer to other clumps and at times further away from them.

Sometimes the closeness invited compatibility, but sometimes it didn't. Sometimes there seemed to be a need for control, or for dominance with clump-styled pushing and shoving, sometimes subtle and sometimes not so subtle.

The mushroom clump understood that there was always more to learn, more to take in and more to understand. It hoped for understanding of the energy of love at love's deepest levels.

Finally the mushroom clump noticed that over the long span of time, it had become one with its natural environment so completely that there was difficulty for it even to breathe in and out, clump-manner, because it was so moved by the realization.

Unfortunately that set it even further apart from other clumps, but then it realized that other clumps had in their own way become one with the particular environments in which they had chosen to live, and that environments and microenvironments were different from one another even though differences might be minute and difficult to discern.

The natures of time and space and space-time were remarkable and had served all of the clumps well, even those that had perished over time, as they had lived as best they could during the time that they'd had and then had given themselves back to the forest carpet. New variations were born, some compatible with existence and some not, but all was as natural as the sighing of a passing breeze. If great storms or endless droughts were to come, some clumps would not survive, but others would.

The mushroom clump watched as the moon set, the sun rose, and set, and the moon rose again.

The High Road

Darkness crept upon them as they made their way higher up the steep, narrow, dirt path, around hairpin turns that brought them to edges that took their breath away when they looked back and down. They saw how far up into the mountain ridges they'd trudged in only one day. They were tired from several days of travel and burdened by the heavy packs they carried, plus simple tools, shovels, an axe, and more fundamental necessities roped tightly to their packs. They moved slowly and methodically.

Sam walked carefully along the path, making his way as methodically and efficiently as he could. He was in the lead, followed by the others who had also made their way out of the valley they'd known as home for their entire lives. Occasionally someone came up alongside him, and they visited briefly.

"How're you doing? Making it along ok?" asked Sam, of Lemuel, his elderly uncle who was struggling because of age and developing arthritis from years of hard work in the fields.

"Sure, I'm doin' all right," Lemuel said, puffing a little.

"We'd better stop for the night soon because it's getting dark," said Sam. "We don't want everybody to walk up this steep path in the dark. It isn't safe."

The small group of women and children trudged along without engaging in small talk. Sam's wife Joan looked around at her children to see how they were and that they were still close to her. Emma, her fourteen year old, was right behind her. Elliot, ten, and Seth, eight, were behind Emma, by now moving slowly, not excitedly looking around as they had done earlier in the day when the group had started out.

Following them were Auntie Ruth, Lemuel's wife, Sam's mother Rosalie, and their neighbors the Goldmans, Ariel, Sharon, and their children Benjamin and Lily. Ben was twelve, and Lily nine. They were good friends with Emma, Elliot, and Seth. The children had all grown up together, had shared cribs, playpens, hide and seek, hiking trails, lunches, birthday cakes, their whole lives, ever since they'd been born. Leaving their homes was extremely difficult for them, and they didn't understand very well why it had to happen.

Emma was stoic at first. "We'll walk on outta here!" But when it came time to actually leave, she cried and whined a little. "Why can't we make it work somehow so we don't have to leave?"

The four younger children were lively or subdued depending on their natural states of mind. They had started this journey by treating it like an adventure, skipping along at first and after a time settling down to walk, but now, after some days of the winding path, they were clearly very tired. The uphill climb was taking its toll.

Up front, Sam stopped at a fairly level place on the path. Both families gathered around, staying close to each other, and spread their blankets on the ground to settle in for the night.

They had moved even more slowly when they'd left their homes some days before. This was because they were leaving their lives behind, lives that they could no longer manage. The reason was an economy that had been failing for many years and taxes that had been increasing for even longer. They had been unable to afford their lives any longer. They had been unable to afford being themselves any longer. Identity had become a luxury item, out of reach.

They needed to find an open area off the path or a place where the path widened enough to allow them to settle into blankets on the ground for the night. They unpacked small portions of the dried fruit and flatbread they'd packed, they chewed slowly, and they drank water from bottles they'd tucked away in small corners in their packs. While they were doing this, they spread their blankets wherever they could and arranged themselves as comfortably as they were able. The slightly broadened path became a makeshift camp.

No one was very comfortable, people were shifting uneasily during most of the night, and people were stretching and pulling themselves up from just past the middle of the night toward early morning. By the time there was a touch of grey in the sky, they were wrapping their blankets into small bundles and stowing them into packs or roping them on, and laboriously they managed to get themselves moving on the way again. It wasn't so much that they were burdened by what they were carrying, or by the void left from all they had lost. It was more as though a group of unanimated, faded shells moved quietly forward. Layers of the wound they had suffered were deep, well into the core of the connection they had with their very existence. Loss was intense. Buoyancy was a luxury fallen by the wayside.

As yet they were unclear about their destination, because they were not heading toward something but were heading away from something else. That left the future hazy and opaque because it wasn't formulated yet. They were tired and in limbo, essences of themselves long since slowly and inexorably extracted and spent over time, as their lives had become less and less expanded and more and more confined. There was no energy to see how the bonds of impoverishment might begin to loosen even if different surroundings could offer potential for a future.

They knew that they had to keep moving toward the ridges that still loomed above them. The path on which they were traveling eventually wound its way up and along the ridges, dipping down briefly into high meadows and shallow valleys until it curved into more hairpin turns as it descended on the other side of the range.

They had been vaguely aware of an extended geography that existed beyond their homes that had been kept in families from generation to generation. Over time, a few individuals had ventured over the mountains and beyond, either on business, or adventure, or because of family connections, or for other reasons. Not all had returned to the security of an environment the intimate knowledge of which was quite naturally intrinsic to virtually everyone in the complex of villages. These were in verdant fields in bottom land of the peak-ringed, enormous valley, or hidden away in pockets here and there, on little mini-valleys built up through millennia where smaller or larger creeks headed down into the valley, tributaries to one or the other of its two rivers.

Some villages were situated on sizeable outcroppings of land that jutted out from steep slopes, usually not far above the valley floor and accessed by picturesque, graceful, wide paths and roads easily seen from the flatlands. Others nestled in meadows near small, hidden lakes, and even a few villages were higher up along sides of mountains, where ancient landslides had formed small plateaus or long vanished waterways had slowed at some point for some reason, had spread out, and had silted in areas that had become fairly flat terraces. Geology that had been laid down and modified by natural forces was interesting, understandable, beautiful, at times mysterious, at times dangerous, but always useful to inhabitants for whom this was home and had been for centuries.

Life was gracious. Wildflowers were abundant everywhere in spring, and meadows were verdant and lush, dotted with grazing livestock and providing fodder that was cut, dried, and stored for winter months. Year round occasional rainstorms ensured steady growth for anything that was cultivated. Distinct seasonal changes meant that there was a time of rest for the soil and for food producing trees, shrubs, vines, vegetables, roots, and anything that provided sustenance for people, domestic animals, and wildlife in the valley.

Because the entire area was more or less hidden away from mainstream societies, a gentle and stable tempo for living had developed, along with an easygoing approach toward one another since all had sufficient of what was needed, and life was good. No one was in a position to feel a sense of impoverishment, for although their lives were on the simpler side, they were not really in need and were able to help one another through times of illness or loss, or whenever someone needed a helping hand.

This is how it had always been. Existence was peaceful. Groupings of people were small, entrenched hierarchies did not exist, and caste systems were unknown. It was a time honored way of life.

Thus, people were not equipped to handle duplicity and greed to any extent. They had not been faced with more of it than what happens within a family, a small village, or gatherings of people from different villages discussing harvests or challenges with crops, such as mildew during very damp years or meager harvests during dry years, or years that for one natural reason or another happened to have shorter than normal seasons.

In the general cycle of life there were always as many different kinds of happenings as there were individuals, but people handled any effects and impacts with the equanimity that stemmed from a pleasing manner of living for as long a time as anyone could remember.

Whatever might be unpleasant, unexpected, uncharacteristic, or limited episodes of violence, emotional upheaval, or hardship now and then were all known and understood, accepted, and handled. They happened as part of the usual ups and downs of existence in this lovely valley. Extremes that might last a long time or develop into a serious, let alone a permanent, change in lifestyles were not reality for the valley and its villages. Until recently, within the last decade.

Further away from the mountains, bustling metropolitan areas grew and expanded, overtaking what had been their suburbs. Those in turn had spread out as populations grew. Eventually, adventurous people, ambitious people, curious people, and occasionally unsavory people moved even further away, a few finally finding their way into the friendly little valley in the mountains.

All of those coming from more heavily populated areas were used to living in a society that was organized but not in the personal way that life in the little valley functioned. They took buses that ran on schedules, they crossed streets in groups waiting for lights to turn green, and they organized their lives without much thought for appreciating their surroundings or enjoying their neighborhood.

Such impersonal ways of living were not understood and gave rise to discomfort for native residents who liked to know who it was who lived next door and whether they had goals or plans that might involve everyone else and that might not be well known or shared. Resentment took seed and grew.

Sure enough, what worked in a more crowded society was out of place and was therefore suspect in the valley. Political and governmental structuring with complex divisions of labor, all of which needed financing, gave rise to costs that the valley folk didn't understand and didn't feel was necessary. Moreover these extra costs left them without the margin of financial safety they had enjoyed through generations.

Those emigrating from more competitive lives and arenas were better equipped for developing ways of living that were similar to those with which they were familiar. And they did. They were the movers and shakers in the peaceful valley. They were also the ones who placed themselves in positions of governmental power and control, because those ways were familiar to them. They thought that by creating systems that might help the valley, they were doing what they understood to be good. It had been good where they had previously lived, but it was not good for the small communities that became obliged to support what had not been necessary before.

Collateral effects blossomed. In any society there were always those who were naturally drawn to power, money, and control, and to those who they thought were the hub of these things. Unfortunately, old families lost a few of their members to the new ideology, leaving the majority hurt and confused, and quite distrustful and skeptical. This is turn led to suspicion between old families who had basically lived in general harmony throughout generations. It also led to the birth of dissidents who opposed what they saw not only as invasive but also as problematic to the point of being injurious and leading to complete collapse of their way of living. A culture was quickly breaking apart.

Possibly, a newer way of life would gradually lose its rough edges and some of its complexities as folks moving into the valley learned to adjust, and an amalgam of old and new would emerge. However, such times are never without hard modification.

Some people evolve in wisdom, some manage to do good things, others take advantage of hard times, some gain, and some lose everything. Eventually an equilibrium might emerge, although small uprisings now and then might occur before a balance might be reached. There would forever after be potential for reversion, for more uprising, and more unrest, because introduction of unfriendly ways of handling difficulties were becoming entrenched and were now a part of everything else. More layers of the food web meant more complex interactions.

Sam's father, Elijah, joined a few others who opposed the newer ways that were developing. He was an outspoken, friendly person who cared deeply for his family and his way of life, for his neighbors and for his village, for his valley and for everyone who lived in it.

Elijah opposed having to pay for what he didn't consider to be necessary, he was in communication with others who were in agreement, and they were gathering information that they eventually planned to present to enclaves of residents in the valley. They were not altogether open about what they were doing, but that was partly because they were by nature a part of the social structure they knew and were already on the taciturn side. Still, as a rule, people were aware who had leanings in any given direction anyway. One evening, on his way to a meeting in a village on a hillside above the valley, Elijah unfortunately fell to his death while traversing a particularly steep stretch of the path.

Sam and his family suffered a deep loss when Elijah died. He had been a force in the family, a rock in the community, and a steadfast, loyal friend in the valley. After his death, disquietude and a rebellious attitude spread more widely among long time residents. After a few more years, after there were two more accidental deaths among people who were in opposition as Elijah had been, groups of people began to leave the valley.

Sam, his family, and the Goldmans were among several groups who left soon after the earliest of the groups. More had followed and more were following. On the face of it, many of the families who had lived in the valley for generations were leaving.

They were the rock solid folk. They were the farmers, the laborers, the teachers, the accountants, the bankers and more, who for many long years had taken good care of each other. They were the people who knew each other, who helped each other, who had grown up together, who trusted each other, and who were familiar with each other's good points, difficult character traits, quirks, and limits.

Quantities and qualities were known and understood.

Everyone did their part, some more than others according to individual personality and character, but everyone did something. Within the beautiful little valley, no one took without giving something. Social mores and productivity to some degree or other existed among all.

No one took something only because he or she was at some level of bureaucracy that existed to enable ways in which it could support itself. No one was removed from the actual interactions necessary for living in communities and on farms. Everyone had always known how people had always functioned in the valley, and detached abstraction was not familiar or understood because folks themselves were the building blocks for how everybody had always lived.

Therefore the increasing confusion that came with the complexity of newer, introduced ideas of organizing local government bewildered and angered the building blocks, who rebelled and then were the ones who left. It turned out to be more of a mass exodus than was thought at first. That began to be apparent when funds that were dependent on those building blocks began to dwindle.

At first, positions that had been created to help support the pyramid of governmental hierarchy began to be cut. Those people found themselves without income, and many were forced to head back to more populated areas where they could find positions similar to those they had lost.

As more parts of government and society continued to be modified in order to afford who and what were still there, people found themselves with lower standards of living, scrabbling to make ends meet, or moving.

There were no extra funds to be channeled to those closer to the top of the hierarchy, and they began to leave too, taking their gains with them. There were plenty of those, because a confusion of complex social systems offered enticing ways to finagle money and favors. Squatters who had nowhere else to go populated houses and land that had been left vacant from the original mass exodus.

The apparently highly functioning new order was fragmenting. It was not sustainable and was decaying, its tendrils no longer nourished by the parent plant whose roots, although still deeply embedded in soil, were dying back from malnutrition. Those participants in the original exodus were hoping to find another environment healthy enough for them to safely take root, and one day, perhaps even flourish again and become reacquainted with who they were and had always been.

They wound their way ever upward on the steep and narrow path that led to the first of many summits, although they could only see the first ridged summit from where they were. They rested around midday and pulled out what sustenance they had with them, parceling it out carefully, leaving enough for the days ahead. Adults were weary with the physical and emotional baggage they carried. The children were quieter now, tired and beginning to feel the burden of a less carefree way of life than they had previously known.

As the day began to come to a close, an especially rocky, steeper, and more narrow section of the path challenged them. They could not see past the immediate hard work ahead of them, but they managed it and with a few last, stAshaous steps, arrived at a small, narrow ridge that was the summit of the first leg of their journey.

They had not known that this was only the first of many ridges, and a sense of despair overcame them. In their exhaustion, they again arranged and settled themselves for sleep, but this time there was a little more room, and the ground was even level in a few places. In the deepening shadows, they nibbled on a frugal meal of bread and dried fruit and gazed into the dusk.

Waning light made them peer out over the view, and they couldn't clearly see ahead toward what would be their future progress for some time to come. They did have a sense of several ridges, wrinkles in the earth, over which they might have to travel. They began to wonder about the valleys that would be nestled in the safety of those ridges, and they wondered about ridges that might be hidden away.

Sam found himself thinking about security and where they could find it. He looked around at his family and friends, and he wondered if they would eventually come across others who had left their little valley before they had. He hoped they would be welcome. He anticipated seeing more friends and acquaintances again, and he automatically began to organize his thoughts toward plans that would prevent many who would come later from finding them.

The difficulty was in knowing who had struggled in reaction to a way of life that didn't suit them, who were free thinkers but also loyal and happy, who were bullies, or basically who were human with frailties and strengths but in the scheme of things would respect others enough to allow them to exist in their own individual ways.

One thing was certain: no one would ever be the same. A tired Sam hadn't yet understood that he was learning, and growing, from what had happened and was happening. They all were. That was inevitable.

Trust and respect, and love, would come as a premium now, but with time a few groups of people here and there would remember how important those were for sustenance of the soul, and would be loathe to bring into their midst practices that might threaten them.

They couldn't go home again and were well into another phase of their existence, seeking new homes. So far they were exhausted, but somewhere within, Sam sensed a faint notion of survival and felt a tiny bit of apprehension dropping away.

A Social Allegory

There was the egg, medium brown and smooth, Nature's perfect oval. I saw how fragile it was, and yet squeezing it end to end was pointless, for it would not break. However, now it cracked along its side, from an inner pressure. The crack grew. A rooster was born.

Having no idea which came first, egg or rooster, I watched with a growing sense of wonder as the rooster stood, stretched, and began to dry. He stepped cautiously forward, then with growing confidence as his limbs strengthened, and he strode outward toward life. I watched.

He was whole, and when squeezed end-to-end he didn't break. A gift from Nature, he was born complete. He grew bolder and walked briskly toward the frying pan.

As he entered the commotion of people, I saw him suddenly recoil. Someone had elbowed him along his side, in the ribs. Now he had a pained, surprised expression on his face. As he backed out and away from the throng, I saw he had his first wrinkle etched deeply into his forehead, a harbinger of more to come when his innate good will was accosted.

Time passed. He carefully began to mingle with the crowd again but not with such enthusiasm as before. He was hungry, he needed sustenance, and he also wanted companionship. There were food vendors among the crowd as well as possible future friends.

He began to perceive who among the people were stronger, and who were subordinate. Here and there he shoved the weaker ones. Either they shoved him harder in return, or they squawked and placed themselves out of his reach.

In this way, he slowly, deftly, day by day, inched his way toward Utopia, where all good people liked to be. In Utopia, there would be room enough for all, with pleasant conversation and much good cheer, and an enormous, long table laden with all manner of good things to eat.

One day, at long last, he came to the long table and sat down to enjoy a well-earned meal. He chatted with those on his left, on his right, and across from him. I noticed that he was enjoying himself immensely.

Time went on. Now I could see that the rooster was in the prime of life. He had discovered that in order to stay in Utopia, he was obliged to defend his place at the table, or someone arriving from the outer limits would want his place. There would be some very animated discussion for a time, with much arm flapping, and now and then some fancy footwork as well. He held on to his place.

Time elapsed. The rooster grew older. I watched as he moved more slowly, although with great dignity.

Then one day, someone from outside shoved in front of him at the table. He was ruffled, and he huffed and puffed, but after receiving a few bruises he backed away. He knew his sojourn at the table had ended. He backed out to the edges of the crowd. I saw him flinch when he recognized where he was, then he bowed his wrinkled head.

Days later, he began to look for food. Hesitantly, prudently, he straightened himself until his back was no longer bent. He found food, old and dry, but he ate. He lived on the fringe that way for some time, growing older, moving ever more slowly.

One day, I saw him settle in the shade of a large, gentle tree, to rest. He rested there often after that, seemingly at peace with the world, but lonely, I thought. The fundamental qualities of the sum total of who he was seemed vaguely translucent, and he seemed to be serenely aware of all that existed around him and further away too. Watching him, I felt rather like an intruder in a domain of soul.

After some days, I noticed he was resting for a very long time. I waited quietly for him to move, wanting to help but not wishing to disturb his well-deserved peace. He didn't move again.

FLIGHT

She sat quietly with her mid-morning coffee, contentedly observing a ray of sunshine as it moved over the stone inlay patio. It eased itself in and out of cracked stonework, Mexican pots full of fuchsia, fern lacework, and a few cacti.

It was too delicate by far for the cacti, she thought. She felt they needed desert sun with which they wouldn't blend but would contrast as simple, sturdy shapes in the glare. Their well-being required direct contact with raw elements, not a protected, leafy niche in a middle class suburban patio. She felt cacti must be very much alive, and she understood why they needed their sharp thorns for competing in their habitat.

Lorraine mused on. She reflected back to her adolescence and young womanhood. What a romantic she'd been, in love with maidenhair ferns and baby's breath. She'd decorated herself with ruffled clothing, with a flower in a buttonhole, and with hairstyles and gestures suitable to a young sentimentalist. After she and Steve were married, she had loved creating light, fluffy pastries and meringues, which, along with espresso, completed the gourmet meals she'd prepared. She felt they'd partaken of much of what she had considered to be the good life. Certainly they had eaten well.

She thought about Steve. He had been so masculine, just the sort of man she'd wanted. He had been protective and had adored her feminine ways. They would sip their before dinner drinks, he usually with his bourbon, she usually with her sloe gin, chattering gently about his future as an engineer after graduation, and about hers as his wife. Her liberal arts education would indeed be a marvelous accoutrement for her as his helpmate, as an enlightened future mother, as an active member of the community in which they would live. She had been excited and challenged. Now she was bored.

In due time they had become established in a smallish suburban community, within easy traveling distance of a fairly large metropolitan area. Weekends they had partaken of friendly Szechuan dinners for two or relished drama at any one of the few small stage-cum-night clubs, or some good jazz, or a critically acclaimed, newly released movie. They had a life that they enjoyed, one that suited their own individual values, or at least they thought so.

As the years passed and their children were born, they acquired a house with enough room for all five: husband, wife, eldest daughter Marcie, and twins Ian and James.

Their home and yard became a hub of many activities. There were always children around, noisy and healthy children playing with building blocks, dolls, trains, skates, tricycles, bicycles, mopeds, all the various interests of children growing from one year to the next. There being many children in the neighborhood, theirs and others' were constantly running to and fro, from house to house, yard to yard.

She took great pleasure in the interior decoration of her home. She became known for being inventive and for having good taste, and she relished the freedom she had in choosing furniture, drapes, carpeting, all those things that showed her own particular stamp of individuality to anyone who was in her home.

Steve allowed her a fairly free budget too, and she settled only for items of better than average quality and craftsmanship. He approved of his wife's handling of his castle. He was busy building his business, and he was doing well.

She had been consecutively involved in Scouts, Girl and Boy, in PTA, as a mother supplying cookies and cakes on demand for school parties, as a homeowner supplying a back-yard for weekend barbecues for the kids, or for Steve and some of their large network of friends, or a rather classy dinner for Steve and his clients.

In the last five years, along with other prominent citizens of the town, she and Steve helped lay the groundwork for and bring to fruition an annual winter series of community concerts. She loved going to these. Although Steve couldn't always make the steering committee meetings, he invariably accompanied her to the concerts themselves – ballet, chamber music, piano, excellent ethnic dancing, a nice variety of delectable happenings in the world of the arts.

She recalled a conversation of a few years ago between Steve and herself. They were enjoying a Grand Marnier in their living room, having just returned from a particularly fine concert. A harpsichordist had played pieces from the early classical era, and they had been lovely, peaceful, so light.

She was quiet and in a pleasant mood, and said whimsically, "Steve, are you happy? Do you like living with me? Sometimes I wonder if you're getting what you want from life."

A startled Steve looked at her and said, "Sure, honey. Can't think of anything more I could possibly want." He paused. "We're secure, settled, we've got the kids, I've got you. I've never stopped loving you."

He gazed at her. "Is that what you mean?"

"Well," she replied, "Sometimes I feel there's a world out there and I don't know anything about it. Sometimes I feel, oh, maybe a little bit shackled. Sometimes I have a yearning to do something totally different – meaningful or ridiculous, I don't know. I know that life is always changing. Social structures change, fashion changes, even morals change, status changes. But I feel I'm staying the same, and I don't want that to happen."

"You still love me, even a little?"

She said warmly, "I love you very, very much. Don't forget that."

Steve smiled, then after a minute said, "Hey, maybe you'd like a hobby. What about checking out some crafts courses at the J.C.? Honey, you're so talented for things like that."

She didn't answer, just looked thoughtfully at him. The moment had passed.

The children were all in high school now, Ian and James freshmen, Marcie a senior.

Marcie was a good daughter, a pretty, wholesome looking person. She was more aggressive than her mother, very busy in school activities, a cheerleader, in school plays, a lively person. She was capable, organized, and Lorraine wondered if she wasn't perhaps a bit bossy at times.

Lorraine loved her daughter but felt as if she didn't know her very well, due more to personality clashes rather than the teenage-daughter-versus-mother syndrome. Marcie often complimented her mother on her good taste and her refined attitudes, but if Marcie felt any detail of her mother's life needed organizing, she would do it, Lorraine's gracious supplications of distress notwithstanding.

Ian and James, although twins, were totally different from one another, not opposite, just very definite individuals.

James played soccer and basketball, got average to above average grades, had Stave's curly dark brown hair, and was an all around cheerful fellow. He was likeable and was usually running off to someone's house or had a group of his friends with him when he arrived home after school. Lorraine found him congenial and easy to be around.

Ian, the more bookish of the two, was also active in school affairs but chose the school newspaper and student body politics as his main interests. He was an intense person, very quick, extremely observant, a person who moved rapidly and forcefully among friends, peer groups, and teachers alike. Weaknesses in personalities nettled him. Ian was physically slightly smaller than his twin. However, one's first impression of him was that he was at least equal in stature to most people. Lorraine was very fond of Ian, and she also wondered if she wouldn't become just a bit shy of him when he became an adult.

All attributes combined, Lorraine decided she had a quite nice family. Throughout childhood she hadn't known how her life would arrange itself and was pleased that it was so pleasant, so rich and well supplied with various interests and causes. True, she would like to see more of Steve, who it seemed was either at work, or at meetings, or in his woodshop working on a cabinet, footstool, or some other household object, or with her at an occasional social activity like a concert.

She would welcome a friend-to-friend relationship with her children and thought that as time would go on, such a relationship would eventually be the healthiest one she could have with them. She also wanted to add a relaxed, close friendship to her relationship with Steve. In fact she felt it was mandatory, as time flies and the children would be out of the house in the not-too-distant future, shaping their own lives. At that point, she and Steve would be alone together. They would have to talk. She was frankly apprehensive.

So Lorraine mused on as she continued to watch her sunbeam cross the patio and highlight her plants. Now, the restlessness she had begun to feel around a year ago was coming into focus. She thought to herself, "Maybe it's finally hitting me. I'm getting old, and I don't like it. I don't like what it's doing to me."

She glanced down at her hands, noticing that they didn't encircle a

cup so gracefully as they'd done ten, even five years ago. The knuckles weren't so smooth. They bulged a little.

"So much for beauty creams," she thought. "Carol said she couldn't find any camouflage at all for aging hands. Cosmetics are mostly for faces. I wonder if older is really better."

Her friend and neighbor, Carol Findlay, and she were in the habit of exchanging coffee breaks every few days.

A few days ago, Carol said, "You know, Lorraine, I don't care about getting old. I don't even care about getting a little fat. I'm happy. Oh, hey, Bob and I are thinking of getting a motor home so we can take off now and then. This'll be when the kids are in college. Doesn't that sound terrific?"

Lorraine, who personally didn't like motor homes, was genuinely happy for her. After Carol left, Lorraine decided she would go into that travel bureau in the shopping center, since she needed to do some grocery shopping anyway. She'd pick up a few brochures.

She was still thinking, checking the sunbeam now and then. "Maybe it's the kids. They don't need me so much now. They're off on their own, even when they're here in the same house with me. Just like Steve."

At that point Lorraine pulled herself up sharply, sitting straight-backed in her chair. It wasn't her children and it wasn't

Steve. It was her. The way they all lived might be a catalyst, but the only person who could help her was herself, and she knew it.

She felt something like the advancing rumble of a mountain summer thunderstorm about to break. All this force was concentrated not in her head but in the pit of her stomach. She felt as though transference of these instinctive feelings from her inner being to her mind, where she could see them, analyze them, and deal with them was literally a matter of freedom or death. She didn't know what kind of death, but she knew it wouldn't be pleasant, since she would still be breathing, sleeping, eating, existing, static.

Perhaps more than anything else, the forceful and unspecified nature of her need to reorganize her value system confused her. She had felt that her role as wife and mother, and she had known that would be her future when she married Steve, was what she wanted to do. She had always realized there would be sacrifices that would encroach on her own time. With three children and a husband, of course there would be sacrifices. That was part of the deal. It seemed her priorities were changing now, and she had to figure out what they were.

No one had demanded she give up any or all of her identity. She had done it on her own, arranging her life to blend with Steve's and to accentuate the lives of her children. She felt she didn't know anymore who she herself was, what she thought, and what she felt. That terrified her.

She was especially disturbed because she knew, deep within herself, that so much sacrifice on her part had not been necessary. She could have lived the same life and simultaneously kept in touch with herself.

But she hadn't. Now here she was, and she had to decide what to do.

"You fool," she told herself. "You'd better look around and find an interest, or you're better off dead."

She decided, "Got to get away and think. I need to know what I think is important." She went inside.

Later in the day, on her patio again, she took a moment to thumb through the pamphlets she had selected at the travel bureau. She paused at one that described the natural, wild scenery and ancient Indian traditions of northern New Mexico. About an hour later, she stood up and stretched. She remained quite still, then turned and moved quickly from the patio into the house.

Three days passed, during which time Lorraine was quiet on the outside, but planning her move, arranging plane schedules and travelers' cheques. On the afternoon of the third day, she was in her room with a freshly made glass of iced tea, when Marcie arrived home after school.

She called out loudly, "Hi, Mom. Where are ya? Hey, can Kathy and I make cookies? For after the game Friday night. She'll be over in a few minutes."

"Sure", answered Lorraine, looking from her bedroom into the hallway at Marcie. "How was school?"

"Oh, OK. Busy though. We have to learn two new cheers

before Friday, and boy, is that new girl, ya know, Josie, boy is she ever slow. I guess it'll turn out OK. We've got two more days to practice. What've you been doing all day?"

"Planning my trip. I'm going to New Mexico for a while."

"Oh. What'd you say? Did you say you're going to New Mexico? Ya mean one of those weekend bus tours, like you and Mrs. Findlay take once every few years."

"No, I'm going by myself on a trip to New Mexico. I don't know yet exactly where, or how long I'll be gone. I want to be away for a while."

There. There. It was out. At last she'd said it out loud. She wanted to be away from her family, she didn't know for how long, and she was beginning to be able to not feel horribly guilty about it.

"What's *wrong*, Mom? *Why*? What for?" wailed Marcie.

Just then Ian came in through the door, followed by James. They arrived home at the same time for once. Marcie told them the plan their mother was making.

"You can't be serious, Mom," came from Ian.

"What're we gonna do when you're not here?" This was James.

After pleas and bargaining came to no avail, the three children finally started questioning Lorraine. They grilled her. They tried every form of manipulation they knew how to use. Why? What were the reasons for her wanting to leave? She didn't love them. She must not care for them. How could she do this to them?

She was crying, but she remained repetitious. She needed time for herself, and she wanted to become acquainted with herself and find out what she wanted to do with the rest of her life, when they were out on their own, and their father was busy working. She wanted to hurt no one. She was sorry about this being such a shock to them, and she wished she could help them understand.

While feelings were being laid bare, emotions uncovered, Steve walked in, home from work for the day. He was quickly filled in by three anxious faces.

He took several steps into the kitchen where they were pacing, milling about, or standing tensely. He grew pale and became rather white. He spoke seriously but firmly, and with a good deal of anger for backup.

"What have I not given you that you should treat me like this? You say you want to find yourself. Goddammit, you're not a member of the lost generation. You're my wife. That's who you are. Don't you know that?"

Lorraine nearly faltered then. Steve was basically not an angry person. She didn't know how to handle his anger. She wasn't accustomed to it. She mentally closed her eyes and hung on for dear life to her decision.

Later on, after a dinner that was scarcely touched, after the children were busy with their friends, stereos, and books, Lorraine brought fresh coffee into the den where Steve was busy with work he had brought home. She caught him at his desk contemplating the paneled wall before him and saw the pain in his expression.

"Here's fresh coffee, love,"

He accepted the mug, cradling it in his hands.

"Why, Lorraine? I've been trying to understand, but I just can't. God knows I don't want you to go, but I don't know how to change your mind. I don't know what I've done to make you feel you need to leave. I truly thought you had everything you wanted."

She said in a low voice, "Steve, it's not you. It's not all the things I have around me. I love you. I love our children, too. Lord, I wish I knew how to explain it."

She paused.

"I just need time to myself. Otherwise, I won't be able to function very well any more. People aren't usually successful with living if they don't know what they want or how to go about getting it. I just want some time to figure out what I want."

He said, "It's so hard for me to understand. I figure when you live, you live."

She replied, "It has to do with the quality of how you're living."

"Then I really don't understand," he said, his hands making a futile gesture. "I thought you had all the quality you needed right here in out home."

"So I do," she said. "It has to do with feelings within me, not with things I have around me."

He stared at her. He looked irritated, and puzzled. He sighed. "I'd better finish this work. Let's talk about it later, OK?"

"OK." Lorraine left the room.

None of the five family members ever forgot that evening. No one would agree with, or actually listen to, Lorraine. All were hurt, all reacted individually. Steve was angry and taciturn. Marcie was pushed out of shape. Sharp-eyed Ian accepted Lorraine's decision more easily than the others. James felt intense betrayal.

Husband and wife did talk on several occasions over the next three weeks. They talked circles around the issue of her taking a trip, but Steve seemed only to see that she was leaving. He didn't seem able to accept her reasons for it, and he didn't seem able to even hear them. He thought them vague and, if the truth were known, unnecessary. Of the children, Ian maintained his composure better than the others, who picked and whined.

On the day of her departure, at the airport, her husband gazed at her, saying, "I guess this is it, huh? Just like that."

He snapped his fingers and gave her a twisted smile. "Lots of luck, honey."

She saw the hurt and bewilderment on his face.

"Bye, Mom," said Marcie. She didn't say any more. She only darted a look at Lorraine.

James stared at her, just saying, "Bye."

"Have a good flight, Mom." Ian was looking directly at her, then glanced away at the departure gate, through which people were now quickly moving.

There were quick embraces. She held back tears and

waved them goodbye as she walked down the boarding ramp to her waiting plane. She was hurt inside and guilty. She'd received little support or best wishes from her family. No one had wished her a good trip. And she knew very well that she was walking out on them.

She was amazed that no one had noticed her restlessness of the previous years, her dissatisfaction with simple daily activities, or her own anger. She was astounded at the lack of communication that had existed within those walls she considered home.

She was also excited and very frightened. She had told her family she didn't know when she'd be back, but she felt they didn't take seriously the fact that she might be gone for a long time, maybe a year or two, or more. She didn't know. She settled herself in her seat and thought for a moment of arid country and cacti.

The Marriage

Jamil walked leisurely along the road, a wide, very dusty road, at dusk. He was wearing only a dhoti and headband, no shoes and no jacket, even though it was late in the year. Traveling at his shoulder, shuffling along, was his water buffalo. She was sleek, not fat, but sturdy and healthy, and placid and contented as so many water buffalo are.

They moved steadily along one of the main roads leading northeast from Old Delhi. Noise was everywhere. People were hawking wares, their displays stretched in a solid mass all along the side of the road. Yet the late-fall, onset-of-winter quality of the dusk hushed everything.

There were fires lit along the roadside, with old, fat, black tea kettles sitting on the coals. Wood smoke, the pungent odor of samosas, and a thousand other smells hovered as near manifestations in the soft air. People were just beginning to bring out shawls and turbans, if they had them. Jama Masjid loomed massive and dusky red in the background with clusters of shopkeepers set up around its base.

On the outskirts of Delhi, Jamil met a friend, Ramlal, who came from his own village. His friend was coming into town on an errand to relay a message from his wife to two of her cousins, about an upcoming wedding.

Before becoming too involved in greeting and conversation with his friend, Jamil turned to his water buffalo, checking her to see that she was not overly tired yet ready to pause for a moment. He gently, absent-mindedly scratched behind her ears as he turned back to his friend.

"Namasthai!" He clasped his friend by the shoulders, smiling broadly, his milk white teeth gleaming in the dusk and whites of large, dark eyes and vivid, although rather soiled dhoti looking nearly iridescent against his dark body in the waning light.

Ramlal returned his greeting, embracing him, slapping him jovially on the shoulder. He was more slender that Jamil and had more delicate features, almond eyes, and high cheekbones. He had a nervous habit of peering down his slender nose at his beautiful hands, which he slowly clasped and unclasped.

He and Jamil began to speak animatedly to one another but their conversation was not loud. Graceful gestures accompanied their conversation, along with heads nodding and wagging.

"Jamil, how goes it? Did your beast work well for you today? Did they like her milk? If they did not, they are too fussy. She is a fine animal, and anyone would be proud to own her."

"Ah, Ramlal, stop, please," chuckled Jamil. "Of course she worked well, and naturally they found her milk fresh and quite wonderful. And now, my friend, how are you? I've not seen you this past week, and I'm concerned. Have I done something to offend you? That would grieve me, you have done so much for me."

"No, of course you haven't offended me," Ramlal spoke less excitedly, and he had a troubled expression on his face.

"I am more worried for you and Asha, that's all. It's the same problem, but I think it's getting worse. My elders are speaking more openly now about the two of you, and what they're saying is harsh. They are so rigid, Jamil. I think they will never accept a marriage between you. They want Asha to marry a Brahmin like herself, not a poor, hard-working Muslim like you. She is my sister, you are my best friend, and I fear for you both."

"Ramlal, such a kind friend, I do not deserve your friendship. What audacity I have, to fall in love with your sister."

"They've told most of the family now, Jamil. Nearly everyone is aware that the two of you wish to be together. I'm sure our entire village knows it. I think life is becoming less safe for you, daily. What about your family?"

"They are quiet, they say little. I feel they are not happy, but they are not incensed as your family is. They live a peaceful life, and I believe they wish the same for me and the woman I choose to be my wife. At least I hope so."

Jamil continued, "The only one who doesn't like my not choosing a Muslim woman is Mehmoud, my younger brother. He has backed away from me, and sometimes the glances I catch from him startle me, they're so intense. But then he's young and rather foolish anyway."

"I wouldn't worry too much about Mehmoud," interjected Ramlal. “He is a political firebrand, an emotional soul, but he is loyal. If you and Asha are able to marry, he may be bitterly opposed. But I think it won’t last long. Then he’ll be even more bitterly opposed to your enemies.”

Ramlal chuckled and continued. “Your family is certainly an interesting lot. If I were a Muslim and you were a Brahmin, I know we would still be best friends. It just doesn’t matter.”

Jamil was gesturing agreement.

Ramlal added, “Seriously, Jamil, I begin to think it might be safest and less burdensome if you were to be married quickly and quietly, without ceremony, since some of the sentiment at a large wedding might provoke violence.”

“Interesting you should say that, Ramlal. The last two evenings, when Asha and I have been able to meet here in town, thanks to your initiative in bringing her on some pretext even though I haven’t seen you, we’ve discussed exactly that. We think it’s what we might do, and we’d like to speak with you about it tonight. Where is Asha?”

Ramlal waved rather aimlessly in the direction of a cluster of merchants with their wares, in a clump at one side of the next intersection.

A girl emerged from the crowd and walked toward them. Her plain cotton sari was neat and very clean, though now a sky blue whereas it has once been royal blue. It was beautiful and soft against her very dark, supple skin.

Her skin color was darker than that of Jamil. That was

one of the main problems in this match, according to his family. It was another barrier to contemplate and overcome.

She reached them, smiling broadly, a delicate, dimpled smile, greeting them with hands pressed together, touching her forehead.

"Namasthai, Jamil," she said, her voice surprisingly deep for a slender, young girl. She was seventeen. She and Jamil both felt they shouldn't wait too long to marry, as time was passing.

"Hello, brother. Once again you have done a beautiful thing by bringing me here. Jamil, we must name our first son after him. He has done so much for us."

Jamil blushed. He was not as forward as Asha. In fact she had wanted to run off last evening, leaving family and friends to circumstance, to be with Jamil. He was more cautious, foreseeing a very difficult life for them if it were devoid of family, immediate and extended.

"Jamil, I thought for a long time today, and I think it's best for us to be married as soon as possible. My parents told me this afternoon that they have gone to a marriage broker, and that my husband would be chosen within a few weeks. They have already consulted our astrologer and given his reflections to the broker. We no longer have a choice."

"Ah, Asha, you will still choose me? The blessings of Allah are bestowed upon me through you, beloved."

Without pausing, keeping on task, she continued. "We need to prepare ourselves right away. We must leave, and we must leave quickly."

Jamil turned to Ramlal. "Brother, will you help? You are the person we want most to be with us at our wedding. Can you bring Asha into town again tomorrow evening? We can go to the muezzin at Jama Masjid. He can arrange our marriage, and he will be able to get proper papers for us."

"I think we want a government official to be present," mused Asha, "Because I'd like to have his signature as a witness on our marriage certificate."

"Good idea," Ramlal approved. "Asha, you must pack tonight. I'll arrange for a village boy to take your things to town after it's late into the night. I'll think of some story to tell him, so he won't ask questions. I wonder where they can be left."

"Leave them with the muezzin," said Jamil. "He'll watch them until we fetch them."

They stood off the side of the road and spoke among themselves for a while longer, finalizing plans. They would meet at the entrance to the inner court of the mosque, from where they would go to the rooms of the muezzin.

After the ceremony, Jamil and Asha would go immediately to the station and take a train to Patna. Patna was several hours away to the northeast. They wouldn't know anyone, and they felt Jamil could find work there. They, who had lived all their lives in a small village, were traveling blindly to another planet called Patna.

They separated, brother and sister to return home, Jamil to arrange things with the muezzin and to buy tickets. In order to pay for the tickets, he sadly sold his water buffalo to the muezzin, who would resell her to one of many men who needed a livelihood and who would pay for her month by month and treat her well.

Such an arrangement was easy for the muezzin. He was the pulse of the large Muslim community in Delhi. He had feelers everywhere.

Jamil would go home later, pack his things, and leave early in the morning. He often left early for town, and there would be no cause for alarm.

The next day, Jamil spent most of his time in and around the mosque. Early evening, at the appointed hour, he met Ramlal and Asha at the entrance agreed upon.

"You are so beautiful." He looked at Asha. "Thanks be to Allah, you love me, too."

"Yes," said Asha. She was radiant, her faded blue sari only adding to her beauty by providing such contrast between something old and faded and something new and vibrant.

"We must hurry, Jamil." She beckoned toward a small antechamber in the wall a short way across the inner courtyard.

"Ramlal," Jamil said softly, "You will soon be my brother officially, and that makes me so very happy. You know we will miss you dearly. Can't you arrange some excuse and come to see us in Patna? At least once in a while."

"I'll see what I can do," replied Ramlal, as they passed through the door into the antechamber. They found themselves blinking and peering around the room. It was dusky in comparison with the glaring autumn sun outside, still far above the horizon in early evening.

A sudden movement to the left caught Jamil's attention, and he swung around. He looked directly into the eyes of his brother, Mehmoud. He thought briefly, incongruously, how sad their expression was.

"Mehmoud! You startled me. What are you doing here?" Jamil asked.

"Oh, Mehmoud, you've found out." Asha was tentative. "We are in love. Can't you please, please be happy for us?"

Ramlal began to back slowly toward the outer door. Mehmoud had said nothing, his sturdy frame reposed in an apparently relaxed slouch.

Now he spoke quietly, resignedly, "A pretty woman and your head is turned. I understand that. But how can you forsake your faith? You and I .... Oh, I thought you were true to Allah. How can you become a worshipper of idols?"

Jamil gasped. "You're wrong, Mehmoud. I am a Muslim. But it doesn't matter. We are just people like everybody else, and we love each other."

He went on, "You see for yourself where we are getting married – a mosque."

And he asked, "Who told you this?"

"Someone who believes in remaining true to his heritage, like I do, although he is Hindu," replied Mehmoud.

Then with a look of growing confusion, Mehmoud

turned to face Ramlal. "Is this true? Did you lie to me?"

Ramlal, who had been listening, moved quickly toward the door.

Mehmoud went after him, a flash of steel in his hand.

"You murdering swine! You wanted me to do your dirty work for you. You filthy bastard!"

Ramlal put his hands in front of himself. One of them clutched a stiletto. He crouched.

Asha cried out, "No!"

But he grappled with Mehmoud, who had reached him and had swung for his throat.

They fought for a brief moment, then they fell back from one another.

Mehmoud grasped his left shoulder tightly with his right hand that was still holding the bloody knife and leaned back against the wall for support.

Ramlal sank to the stone floor. He was bleeding freely from a gash in his throat.

He looked blankly at Asha and whispered thickly, "I had to protect you. Don't you see? You're a Brahmin."

As Asha moved toward him, his head slowly rolled to the side, his eyes began to glaze, and they heard the unmistakable sound of his death rattle.

Jamil supported Asha, who began to sob in deep gasps.

They both moved in a daze toward Mehmoud. He had a bad shoulder wound from a puncture and a gash, but with help he would eventually be all right. Jamil began to wrap the wound with a shirt from his bundle of clothes that he had found in a corner of the antechamber.

Mehmoud spoke slowly, with effort, "Go now, hurry. Be married quickly. Hurry! Go, may Allah be with you."

Overwhelmed and in a state of shock, sobbing, they couldn't speak, and numbly followed Mehmoud's urging, heading inside. There was no way back now, only forward.

When they emerged only minutes later, there were no traces of their brothers. They hurried away to catch their train.

Raptors

They built their nests with sturdy sticks and brush and gently lined them with soft mosses, bits of fluff from plant seeds and animal fur left over from shedding. They kept close watch on each other and on their neighbors, to be certain that there was adequate space from nest to nest and that the cliffs and crags separating them were sufficient. They looked left, right, down, and up when calculating the space they required. Their neighbors were doing the same.

It was an exquisite dance, each pair understanding the intricacies of the latticed whorls of space they occupied, each pair assessing their strengths and weaknesses, one from another, and each pair ultimately claiming what they could protect. Once boundaries were subtly understood, there was only the occasional attempt by an outsider to claim space. The truce might have been seen as uneasy but it really was quite straightforward.

Other species harassed one or more of the pairs as they gathered nesting material, and then after a time, as one gathered food for the other and then for the chicks.

It was part of the whole.

Eventually the chicks took stumbling steps, then stretched their wings, and after a time learned about air currents and wing muscles as they clung to the edges of the nest and began to grow familiar with the world. They saw how their parents observed space, never stopped observing space. The chicks learned about space too.

A time came when, one by one, surviving juveniles from nests in the area stood at the edge of their own personal abyss and launched themselves into it, flapping and soaring, with knowledge they had assimilated by watching their parents. Nearly all juveniles flew away and began to take the responsibility for their own lives. All was as it should be.

Until their home territory was forever lost.

Undertones

An extremely hot afternoon developed into a sultry evening with air that was thick and difficult to breathe. Some evenings in the early summer heat are pleasant although not necessarily easy to navigate, because they feel like small walls are everywhere and are always in the way. Relaxing into them feels something like being in a hazy comfort zone.

This particular evening was not pleasant that way. Although it wasn't muggy, it had elevated itself to a fog of hindrances because it had become a barricade to free movement. It made simple thoughts a challenge. Laughter was out of the question, and optimism was not about to happen.

A certain dullness of spirit seemed to permeate everything and everyone. Normally open minds had closed down as a defense mechanism. Cheerfulness had flown out windows and doors, not to be chained down by the oppressive atmosphere.

Probably the worst part of it was the dark corners that seemed to come into some kind of bas relief. Everyone has some dark corner somewhere, generally kept in check by common sense, courtesy, and even simple good manners, just as every building has a dark shadow or unseen corner somewhere inside. Those aren't normally on exhibit, so others might not know what they are or what might trigger their emergence.

The evening didn't hold triggers, and it didn't encourage displays of outbursts, whining, slow anger, devious maneuvers, lies, or anything else that might exude from dark corners. Instead, these behaviors retreated into even darker recesses and stewed there.

Angela sensed the underlying threat, although she didn't know how to express it. She felt pushed down, and her mind wasn't able to breathe. Her automatic reaction was to hide herself away from interacting with others. It was defensive posturing, but the idea of it seemed to help.

She said "Hello" to neighbors when she came out to the front yard after dinner and dishes, and she was almost tentative about it, but for some reason she felt safer that way. Safer from what, was a mystery. She had no idea what. She liked the neighbors.

Mr. Owens across the street was trimming his lawn, and Mrs. Yablonski next door to Mr. Owens was hand watering her flowers along her front walk. She finished that and set a sprinkler in the middle of the smaller of her two front yards. Meanwhile Mr. Owens was cleaning his trimmer to put it away, having finished what he'd been doing.

Next door, the Zimmermans were relaxing on their front porch. Mr. Zimmerman put his glass of iced tea on the small table between them and a little lethargically waved an arm in greeting in Angela's direction. Mrs. Zimmerman nodded to her.

The neighbor on the other side was sweeping a sidewalk, or at least it sounded that way. The hedge between the two houses was fairly thick. You couldn't see through it.

Angela's twin nephews, Trevor and Jack, tumbled out the front door with a soccer ball. It wasn't a very large soccer ball because they were only four and a half years old. They loved to play in the front yard. Since theirs and the neighbors' houses were in a cul de sac, they often played in the large circle in the street. However that didn't happen when there wasn't anybody right there to watch them, and it usually happened only during evenings when folks in the neighborhood were at home and were busy outside, not driving somewhere.

Even though they were small children who loved to play, they were quieter than usual, too. The evening had permeated their psyches as well.

Angela watched them. She saw that there was no one around them, no cars in the area, and the neighborhood was home and out front.

Angela was protective of them.

She lived with her mother's sister and husband, Joy and Michael, and Trevor and Jack. She had moved in with them three years before, after her parents had been killed in a sudden traffic accident one evening. She was an only child. She had been eleven then and had had nowhere to go.

Her family and extended family had always been close. Joy and Michael had wanted her to come to them, there had never been any question, and she'd moved in with all her things.

Their house was large enough, and she had her own room.

Trevor and Jack had been one and a half, and Angela had fallen into a helpful routine with them that quite naturally continued as they grew and as she began to adjust to loss and a different way of daily life. Actually it wasn't that different, because her mother and Joy had been close sisters with similar values, even in the way they ran their households.

She missed her parents. At first it was hard not being able to see them and be with them. After a few years, she had begun to adapt and with a fair amount of grace, to accommodate the feelings her memories brought out. It seemed to be more about getting used to the way things were now, and she was growing into that.

Once in a while, out of the blue, pain from the loss and emotional trauma of that time surfaced with such suddenness and force that it left her breathless. Usually she felt a sort of unconscious aching that seemed to hover just out of reach. Even that was becoming easier to handle and sometimes, she couldn't even find it.

She didn't want to forget her parents and fought herself when memories seemed to be fading. Joy and Michael were wonderful about that. During those difficult times, they'd pull out photo albums or video clips, and they'd all thumb through photos, talking about good times, and watch video clips. It felt bittersweet, but it helped. She didn't realize how much it helped Joy also, but she was aware that it did help.

Such a major loss needed time for adjusting. The rough

corners had rounded over time, and everything seemed a little smoother now. Not gone, but smoother, Angela thought. She wasn't able to voice her thoughts about this very well, mostly because she didn't consciously know them herself. She realized that this would change over time.

She experienced plenty of angry moments wondering Why? Why her parents? Why her? Why Joy and Michael? Why would her nephews grow up without knowing their aunt and uncle?

She hadn't learned to direct her anger very well yet, but she found that helping her two nephews brought relief from unsettled feelings. She loved them unconditionally.

The anger seemed to be less intense now. She seemed to have shaken some of it off, as though she were shaking off excess water after climbing out of a swimming pool. Or maybe she was growing tired of it and was instinctively beginning the process of adapting to loss.

As the boys played with their small soccer ball, Angela felt her brownish blond bangs sticking to her forehead and felt beads of moisture at the back of her neck under her hair, even though she wasn't moving or exerting herself. The evening seemed to be attacking her, leaving her feeling unpleasant physically and emotionally.

She saw that the two small towheads in the street were glistening also, foreheads and even forearms. She called to them to slow down. They hadn't been moving that quickly, but they didn't need to overheat. There was already that hostile feeling in the air. Acting on the side of safety was better.

She moved a sprinkler closer to the sidewalk and turned it on, inviting them to run through it for a few moments so they'd cool down. She curled herself into a comfortable place on the lawn and watched them.

Her mind began to drift, and before she could stop it, she was back answering the door, right here at this house where she had been staying, when the police had come to tell her and the family about the accident. It felt so real, as though it were happening for the first time, yet all over again.

Trevor and Jack laughed and screamed happily as they threw the soccer ball around the pavement and into the sprinkler, following it into the water. They broke through her thoughts and brought her back from the dark place into which she had wandered. She saw that they were all right and were enjoying themselves. They were beginning to move a little slower now, they were soaking wet, and abruptly, they ran to her and plopped down by her side. They were panting a little.

After a few moments, they began to fidget and squirm, but there wasn't the impetus of children who are suppressing energy. It was more like children who have been drained of any liveliness, who don't even know where to look to get any of it back. Usually it bubbles up in children, bringing its exuberance into their hearts. This evening there didn't seem to be any room for bubbles, and even if there were bubbles, there wouldn't be enough lightness of air to keep them moving up, up, and away.

They'd remain in place and break with a light crackle or simply fade away.

Angela shivered for no reason and gathered up the boys and their soccer ball, herding them toward the front door. They weren't quite dripping any more, and she knew that it was time for their baths and then bedtime. She felt a strange need to get them inside where they would be safe. She noticed without thinking about it that the neighbors were wandering toward their doors, too.

It was an unconscious compulsion, but it was strong enough for her to marshal herself to reach for the faucet and turn off the sprinkler. She managed that and found herself pushing the boys through the front door, quickly following them and closing and locking the door behind her. She wasn't aware of locking the door.

Michael was relaxing in his favorite chair, watching the evening news, and Joy came in from the kitchen, untying her apron and putting it on the counter behind her. She quickly glanced around for the boys whom she shepherded up the stairs for their baths and called down to Angela, asking her if they'd been running through the sprinkler.

Angela said, "Yes," and offered to help with baths.

"No, honey, but thanks anyway. I've got it."

Angela went over to the dining room table where she picked up a schoolbook and began to do her homework.

At first, she didn't hear the very light scratching on the

outside of the front of the house. She had opened her history book and was reading the chapter assigned for the next day, and she was engrossed in a description of how people had lived in early America before the Revolutionary War. How did they do it, she wondered, coming all that way on a wooden boat, chopping down and hewing the lumber they needed to build their homes, keeping an ox or a horse so it could pull a plow for a field needed to grow food, all the while finding shelter and gathering food while they were setting up a homestead.

She loved history. She was drawn to the wagons and harness she saw in the county museum and to old, hand sawn boards and huge hinges on large doors of old barns that were still standing in fields just outside of town. She wondered how it felt to do these things yourself, by hand, when that was the only way to do things. You couldn't make the choice to follow older customs rather than use newer machinery, because newer machinery hadn't been invented yet.

The old ways felt precious, knowledgeable, and with a value all their own. She didn't think about a slower pace of life simply because building something and doing what was necessary for that took more time. Her reflections tended toward the idealistic, romantic version of life in the slower lane.

She also suspected that the knowledge and craftsmanship that resulted in buildings lasting down through centuries were far older than what was built in the New World, or maybe in the Old World, or anywhere else for that matter. She would have loved to follow a craft back through time and see where it had originated, who had contributed to it, and why ever it might be fading out. How could anything of such importance be allowed to fade away?

She didn't know that much about any of these things, but her mind and more important, her spirit accepted the truth of timeless craftsmanship. She wanted to know more.

Occasionally she felt a sense of timelessness. It was probably one reason she was acutely alert to the feel of the evening, without consciously realizing it. There was something timeless in the unease and whatever caused it, as though the reason behind it had existed through millennia, in the ethos.

Her view of the world sometimes took on too much of a surreal, romanticized inclination. And yet her fight-flight mechanism was activated.

The scratching grew more distinct. Michael looked up and met Angela's glance toward the door. She seemed to be shivering for some reason, although the evening wasn't chilly. He also felt a little unsettled at the sound, although he figured there was probably an animal outside. Probably a raccoon, he thought, following its nose to what was still in the air from the mac and cheese casserole they had eaten for dinner.

The scratching seemed to be moving along the outer wall, even heading around the corner to the side of the house where the kitchen was. It was an off-and-on scratching, mostly light, like something being barely drawn along the outside of the building. Once the sound seemed to have passed more toward the rear of the house, it faded.

Neither of them thought about the vines that climbed the outer wall along that side. Even if they had remembered those vines, a raccoon couldn't come through closed windows upstairs, wouldn't even want to move past the area where it could smell casserole.

These barely conscious explanations coming out of the rational mind lulled Michael into an acceptance of the slight scratching sounds, although there was a disconcerting unease in the air, and Angela seemed to be nearly poised for something a little like escape or defense. Michael couldn't guess what and said nothing at all. Angela felt it but she didn't know what it was. It was lying vaguely out of reach of her conscious mind that was involved with her history lesson.

Joy toweled off the boys who were climbing out of the bathtub. They were clean, faces, hands, feet and bodies freshly soaped and rinsed, and hair soft and dripping. Joy finished by rubbing their hair in the large, soft towel she was using. Clean pajamas were on a bathroom shelf where she'd placed them, she grabbed them, separated them, and pulled them on the boys.

They brushed their teeth under her watchful eye and were ready for bed, but they were still wide awake although not very lively. They had played hard, but the character of the evening still affected them. All three headed to the boys' bedroom, and Joy tucked each into his own bed, arranging the covers and settling them in.

Tonight was Michael's turn to read them their bedtime

story. Joy left the boys' room and headed downstairs, calling that the boys were ready. He met her on the stairs, went on up and headed into the boys' room, picking up a book from the catchall desk near the doorway. He settled into a chair next to it, near the small baseball-decorated table lamp there, opened the book, and began to read them the story about a friendly dragon that saved the world.

They were clapping their hands and exclaiming, because they liked this story. They flapped their arms and flew with the little dragon as he flew from city to city and instead of starting fires, put them out, one after another, because he could breathe ice if he wanted. Being a good natured, helpful dragon, he did breathe ice. The boys huffed and puffed right along with him.

Then all the fires were out, and the dragon was thanked by the king who gave him a forest of his own, near a small farm where his friend, the farmer's son, lived. Everyone lived happily ever after.

By this time the boys were quieter. They usually clamored for "Another story, Daddy! Another story!" but this evening they seemed to be drifting peacefully into drowsiness.

Michael went to their bedsides and kissed each good night very lightly and quietly on their foreheads, walked softly to the door, setting the book back on the pile of books on the desk and switching off the table lamp. He pulled the door nearly closed and made his way to the stairs.

He took the first few steps and heard the slight scratching. It was close by, outside along the second story outer wall, and it seemed to be headed along the wall again, only this time it was upstairs, not downstairs. Michael was more curious than alarmed, but this time there were no thoughts that minimized it or pushed it away. He did wonder what this could be.

He walked to a large window at the end of the hallway and looked out. He didn't see anything. He looked up, down, and to either side. He still didn't see anything. He stayed still and listened.

There it was, the slight scratching, moving along the outer wall just around the corner from where he was standing. It was probably near his and Joy's bedroom, the first room off the upstairs hallway. It was still moving.

Next to their bedroom was a bathroom that didn't have a door to the hallway, because they had claimed it as a master bath. It could only be entered from their bedroom. Some minor construction was all that had been needed. It wasn't especially large and didn't have a tub, only a shower, but it was enough.

The boys' bedroom came next. It was a fair sized room, and after it, the hallway ended with another large window. The two windows at each end of the hallway allowed cross ventilation during summer months and let in natural light all year round.

Angela's room was across the hallway from the boys' room. Next to that, across from the now walled off bathroom, was another bathroom that was larger and included both a tub and shower. This was where the boys had just had their baths. The stairwell took up the remaining space on that side.

Upstairs was a little smaller than downstairs because the roof began half way up the second story. Part of the bedrooms and bathrooms had slanted ceilings, but there was no crowding because the roof was steep, and slanted walls followed the roof line. Any lost space in any room was arranged for closets plus cubbyholes for storage. Fairly roomy clothes closets were situated in places with maximum headroom, and towels, sheets, and various supplies were tucked away in other storage areas. The design was simple but efficient.

There was enough outer wall space for something to scoot along and make scratching sounds.

Downstairs had a more conventional layout, with a living room, a kitchen in one corner of which was a pantry, the dining area which was a large, open extension of the kitchen, a family room, and a half bath. Rooms were spacious and friendly.

The front door opened into a small foyer with large hooks for winter coats and beneath it, a two-tiered bench divided into cubbyholes for boots and galoshes. The space was small but extremely convenient, and everyone used it with abandon. It was supposed to be a space for organizing, but sometimes clothing and shoes dripped off hooks and shelves when owners were in a hurry or impatient.

It was a space that Michael absentmindedly, automatically checked whenever he came downstairs, because it was where the front door was. This evening, Angela was checking it too.

Still upstairs, Michael listened intently now, because

the scratching seemed to be headed in the direction of the boys' room. He didn't like that and wanted to know just what was causing this scratching. He still wasn't too alarmed but was definitely apprehensive and was puzzled about not seeing, knowing, or figuring out what was making this odd noise traveling along the outer wall.

He stealthily peeked in the boys' door and saw that they had fallen asleep. They looked peaceful. The curtains at their window were open and so was the window, but the screen was locked. At the moment, the only sound he heard was the soft breathing of his children. If scratching were there, he would have heard it through the open window.

Its absence jogged at his peace of mind. Where was it? Was it waiting somewhere just out of sight, along the outer wall?

He wasn't sure what he wanted to do. Well, he *wanted* everything to be normal and all right, but his logical mind wondered where it was, where whatever was making the scratching sound was, because his children were vulnerable.

He decided to step inside the door, sit down along the wall, and watch his sons for a little while. This was something he liked to do now and then. He enjoyed being close to them, being near them while they were so peacefully asleep. He felt like he was a tangible part of their lives at just this moment that he was sharing with them.

He also didn't want to leave them alone. For some reason his sense of security felt shaky. Something didn't feel quite right or quite safe. His nerves felt like a rough board that needs some sanding, and he knew there were splinters there. He wished he could see them, because splinters find their way into your flesh when you aren't looking. He wanted to stay where he was, at least until this jarring sensation passed and he was comfortable about the boys' safety again.

Finally, he slowly and quietly rose and left the room, shutting the door softly, listening intently but hearing nothing. He made his way downstairs, glancing out the window in case the scratching noises and whatever had made them had returned, but there was nothing.

Reaching the family room, he found Joy curled into the soft cushions at the end of the sofa. She was engrossed in a mystery that she was enjoying immensely. She glanced up, smiled, and immediately immersed herself in the story again. Michael was alert to her demeanor, and she appeared relaxed to him.

He saw Angela at the kitchen table, busy with her homework, and noted that she seemed to have lost that sense of unease that she'd had earlier in the evening. Tension was gone from her shoulders, and her neck muscles that had been tightly pulled under the skin only an hour or so ago were relaxed. Her fear or dread, or whatever had been amiss, had faded.

But Michael wasn't convinced. Deep within himself, he knew something was a threat, his perception was that his family was threatened, and he was partly still on alert although he didn't show it, or hoped he didn't. He wasn't entirely conscious of it himself. He couldn't consciously reconcile a scratching noise with a threat, especially since there were plenty of small animals in the neighborhood.

Their cul de sac was the last group of homes before woodlands and meadows began. They lived in the suburbs and were flanked by small farms and older, larger, family farms, complete with their own woodlands and ponds. It was a wonderful setting with opportunities for growing boys to roam when they were old enough for hiking and exploring.

Meanwhile, Michael was aware that critters visited and inhabited their neighborhood, but this scratching along a wall, moving along the outside of the house, didn't seem to fit noise patterns to which he had become accustomed. The underlying question of what was causing it unnerved him.

Joy seemed content on the couch, so he wandered over to Angela who had been uncomfortable earlier.

"Hey, did something really upset you earlier?"

She looked up. "I guess everything's ok now."

He wasn't quite expecting that reply. "So you *were* upset earlier? You looked a little nervous to me but you're calmer now."

She hesitated. Then she said, "It felt heavy or something outside. I was watching the boys and then it just seemed better to come inside. So we did, and we shut the door. I don't know why. It was probably nothing."

But she didn't look as though it was nothing.

"How do you feel right now? Do you feel better?"

"Uh, well, a little better I guess. I don't know. It still feels sort of itchy or something."

"Like something isn't settled or in place, or is different?"

"Yeah!" she exclaimed. "Yeah, it feels like that. But it's weird because I can't tell what it is. I don't know why."

"Why?" She looked right at him. "Did I do something wrong?"

"No, sweetie, of course not. I just wondered. I feel a little funny too, that's all."

"It's about that scratching, isn't it?" Angela asked.

"Yep. I figure there's some kind of critter behind it. That makes the most sense. Some of those guys can crawl everywhere."

He didn't say out loud that he didn't know what could scratch its way all along the vertical outer walls of a house.

Each of them looked sideways at each other. Each knew something was amiss.

Just then, Joy came toward them, heading to the kitchen for a glass of water.

"What's going on?"

"We're just wondering about something we heard earlier, that's all."

"You mean the scratching on the outside of the house." Joy stated it. It wasn't a question.

"So you heard it too?" Michael asked.

"Yes. I heard it when I was giving the boys their baths. I couldn't figure out what it was."

"Maybe an animal," Michael said.

“It gave me the creeps,” said Angela. “I felt funny outside, too. That’s why I brought the boys in a little earlier. We could’ve stayed out a little longer.”

“Was everyone else headed inside?” Joy wondered.

“You know, I guess they were. I didn’t think about it then, but I remember waving to Mrs. Yablonski, and, oh, the Zimmermans were standing up and saying Good Night to everyone. We came in and I closed the door, so I don’t know who was still out.”

They all grew quiet. Joy finished her glass of water and went back to the couch, Michael headed for his chair, and Angela gathered her paperwork together for tomorrow and took a schoolbook into the living room. She sat on the other end of the couch and opened it. No one said anything, but no one felt like being alone.

Michael stood up and said he was going to check on the boys and would be right back. When he opened the door to their room, they were breathing softly and regularly, and he smiled. He returned downstairs and reported that all was well, no scratching heard.

Michael sat down in his chair again, then looked up. Suddenly Angela was standing close to him and Joy, wide-eyed and terrified.

“Something frightened me,” she said in a small voice. “I don’t know what it was, but I’m scared.”

Joy headed toward her and scooped her into a soft hug that had the effect of cradling her and making her feel safe. Angela had had some bad nights in the past, but they had faded in intensity with time. Joy's immediate reaction was to protect her from bad memories and the loss and fear that sometimes accompanied them.

Angela said, "I'm ok but I feel like I did earlier, when everything felt heavy and wrong somehow."

She didn't move away. She felt safe with Joy who had always opened her heart to Angela. Angela was like a daughter to her, but she wanted to respect Angela's feelings of loyalty to her deceased parents. There were delicacies of feelings, but all came from love and caring, and Angela was her daughter now. Michael felt the same.

Michael was hurrying past, to check on the boys again. When he opened their door, he found them wide awake and looking around as though they weren't sure where they were. They looked confused, but they didn't look afraid. Whatever had caused them to wake up apparently hadn't frightened them. They had probably been sleeping soundly like they usually did.

The question that hovered in the air was what had awakened them.

They looked at their father but didn't say anything. He hadn't turned the light on, he was smiling at them, and they were relaxing back into sleep already. One rubbed his eyes and yawned, settling down, and the other was already curling up under his blanket.

Michael listened intently, but he didn't hear any scratching noises that might be just outside. The boys were already drifting off to sleep again. He moved quietly out into the hall but left their door half way open. He didn't want them tucked away in there by themselves. He told himself they wouldn't be so afraid with a half open door, but the truth was that he wouldn't be so afraid that way.

Out in the hall, he listened again. And there it was. The slight scratching was coming from the direction of the window at the end of the hall. It seemed to be very close to the window, and it still seemed to be headed around the outer wall of the house, coming back up on the other side. The next room it would pass would be Angela's.

Michael headed silently and swiftly toward the far window. He found himself avoiding standing in front of it but stayed off to the side, just barely peering out. He automatically kept his own exposure to a minimum while he looked to see what was there.

Nothing was there. Or at least he couldn't see anything, but he knew something was there. Something was outside, and it was checking out his house, his home, and his family. Its threat came from the insidious way it undermined the safety and comfort that should be within the home.

Earlier, it had imparted a sense of foreboding, maybe even of evil, and of danger. It had stolen a precious part of the neighborhood, the feeling of harmony, and had left a sense of apprehension in its place. True, there was only a whisper of these senses and they hadn't been voiced, but they were the kind that people recognized and felt.

Michael didn't know how to proceed, but none of all this was happening on a conscious level in his mind. It was the unease that he couldn't shake, and he knew without reservation that it was affecting Angela, too. Joy didn't seem to feel it as much, or else she was good at hiding it, which helped her nurture the kids. She was naturally protective, and she would be waiting to see his expression when he came downstairs.

When he made his way downstairs, he moved slowly. He reached the bottom of the stairs and deep in thought, trying to come to terms with what he didn't actually know, went past Angela still doing her homework and on toward the couch where Joy was looking up at him. He couldn't read her expression. However she was very good at reading his.

"You're worried," she stated. "You can't figure out why." This was a statement as well. It was the truth, and they both knew it.

"What's going on?" asked Angela.

"I'm not sure," replied Michael, "but I need ask you both something. By any chance, are you guys uneasy about something? Anything?" He almost started to describe what he was trying to figure out, but his sense of needing to protect them stopped him.

They both looked up at him. Joy's look was level to the point of being disconcerting, but Angela's was questioning and fearful.

Angela spoke first. "I didn't like it outside this evening. I don't know why. I couldn't figure it out. I even got nervous and made the boys come in a little early. It was like I had to get them inside and the door closed."

"I never felt like that before. It was a little like after Mom and Dad died, and I wasn't sure why, and I figured someone did it on purpose. I knew they didn't but everything was so scary."

Joy cradled Angela into her arms again. "Honey, we love you so much. We'll always protect you and take care of you." Her voice grew soft. "We aren't your Mom and Dad but we feel like you're our daughter. You'll always be our daughter."

Angela let herself be gently rocked. There were tears on her cheeks. Joy felt them and gently wiped them away.

Michael sat down next to Joy and looked past her at Angela. His voice was full of concern for her, but he still needed to know. "Honey, I know you picked up on the same thing that we did. Do you have any idea what it is?"

He went on, "When I checked on the boys a few minutes ago, they were wide awake. Then they started to yawn and began to fall right back to sleep. I couldn't tell why they were awake. I didn't see anything."

Then he said it. "I didn't hear any scratching there, only at the end of the hall. I don't know if it already went past their room. "

Michael explored his thoughts and asked, "Did either of you feel like there was something that made you feel, well, maybe a little threatened?"

"Yes!" Angela said immediately, and Joy added, "It feels like I need to be sure that Angela and the boys are safe, and when you left the room just now, I listened to be sure that you were ok."

"I don't know why," she added. "It just feels like that."

"Honey, did the neighbors act funny this evening when you were outside?" Michael asked Angela. "Do you think they noticed anything?"

"I don't know. I didn't think about it," Angela said. "I guess they were kind of quiet. Nobody was talking much. It wasn't late but they were headed inside about the same time we were."

"Everybody seemed to be winding down what they were doing at about the same time," she added.

That was odd, now that she thought about it. People didn't normally finish yard work or watering, or their iced tea, at the same time. This hadn't been obvious since people were quiet and moving a little slowly, and then it seemed that they drifted into their homes so you didn't really notice whether they were there or gone.

Michael and Joy looked at each other. They immediately realized what Angela had not. There was a reason for what seemed at first glance like normal behavior and events, but the reason wasn't normal. There was a reason for the vague feeling of threat, of foreboding, and for the scratching. They knew they had to figure out the reason.

They knew that they were in danger. Now they knew that whatever was there would have to leave. They didn't know whether this was an unnatural event of some kind, and it would leave on its own, or whether they would have to make it leave.

They couldn't see it. They could only hear it. And feel its presence.

It was going to be a long night, Michael thought. He wouldn't be able to rest with an unseen threat to his family weighing so heavily. He wasn't sure what to do.

He asked Angela, "Honey, did you feel better when you all came inside earlier? Do you feel something here, now, or do you feel safe?"

She hesitated but then said, "I just went to where I feel safe. I don't know why I still think something's out there. I don't know what it is."

"I don't either," said Michael, "But I'm going to watch for something, anything, so I'll know what to do."

Joy stood up and said she was going to go check on Trevor and Jack again. Michael was watching her and could see her nerves were taut now. He began to check windows and doors.

Angela watched but then pulled out her schoolwork again. She found herself listening to hear footsteps that told her where they both were and waiting for them to return, and she was listening for scratching on the outer walls.

Michael came back into the room, saying that everything was closed and locked and that he hadn't seen anything out of place. Joy came down the stairs and over to where they were, saying that the boys were all right although they were awake again.

She had thought she might bring them downstairs, but

then she rationalized that even though they didn't look sleepy, they were quiet and seemed peaceful and comfortable in their beds. She hoped they would fall back to sleep if they stayed where they were. As long as they were safe.

Michael decided to call a few neighbors to ask if they had noticed anything unusual while they were outside or if they had heard anything after they came in. He figured it wouldn't be a good idea if he immediately started talking about "scratching noises" but better to let them say whatever they felt comfortable telling him.

He decided to begin with the Zimmermans next door. When Fred Zimmerman answered on the second ring, Michael suddenly felt a little silly but quickly remembered the almost startled expressions he'd seen on his sons' faces.

"Hi Fred, this is Michael."

"Hey Mike, how are ya?" Fred said in a friendly voice.

"Say, Fred, I was wondering if you saw anything sort of out of the ordinary this evening. Angela saw you and Shirley outside earlier. She brought the boys in a little earlier than usual. Said you were heading in too."

"Yeah, we saw them. We decided to go on inside about then, too."

"I don't know how to ask this, Fred. I guess I'll just come right out with it. Angela came in because she was a little nervous. She isn't sure why. So I wondered if you and Shirley picked up anything out of the ordinary."

“Uhhhh, well, since you brought it up....” Fred hesitated and then went on, “It feels kinda funny to say this, but when we saw Angela herding the boys in, for some reason we thought it’d be a good idea to go inside, too. Almost felt urgent. Can’t explain it any better than that.”

“Did you guys figure out why, by any chance?”

“No, not really. But we’ve been keeping close all evening. Strangest thing. We figured it was our imagination, but I hafta tell you, we thought there’s something outside.”

“Ok, scratching noises, right?” Michael blurted it out.

“Oh man, yeah, exactly,” Fred replied. “Do you know what they are?”

“No, but it sounds like they’re on the wall outside. They weren’t far from the boys’ bedroom. I guess that’s what made me own up to it and give you a call. By any chance d’ya know about anyone else in the neighborhood?”

“Nope,” said Fred. “I’m really glad you called, because I wanted to know, too.”

He took a deep breath. “Listen, we might have a problem we need to know about. Tell ya what, I’ll call next door to our left and across the street. Can you call in the other direction at the circle? I’ll call ya back in a few minutes.”

“Ok,” Michael said. Fred hung up abruptly, and Michael looked for phone numbers. There were two houses to call, and Fred had two. He wanted to be ready when Fred called back. He had held out a thin hope that things wouldn’t go this way, but there it was, and people needed to know if the neighborhood was safe or if something was wrong.

He phoned the others and spoke with an adult from each household. He briefly described why he had called Fred and recapped the conversation for the others. What did they think would be a good thing to do? He told them he'd get back to them as soon as Fred had called him back.

They were aware, too. They didn't know what it was, but they were uncomfortable. He heard them say what he was feeling.

"It felt like it was just time to be inside. I checked to be sure that we were all inside. I felt silly doing it but it just seemed right."

"I made sure we were all here, and then I checked all the doors and locked the windows too. Gosh, I never lock windows. We always leave them open whenever we can. We like the fresh air, and it helps with the electric bill too."

They were glad he called, they said, and they felt it was important to find out what was going on. They wanted to do something and would be waiting for him to call back. One mentioned checking out the trees and hills behind their cul de sac, and the other wondered if they should call authorities although she had no idea what they might say. She wasn't even sure which authorities they should call, but she'd think about that.

About a half hour later, Fred called back. Joy and Angela weren't hovering near the phone, but they were listening closely.

Fred said, “Yep, they feel it. They want to do something. One of ‘em is sorta wired about it and wants to be gung ho about searching the entire neighborhood, corners an’ all, and the other one wants to talk to everyone about it.”

He went on, “Maybe it’s a good idea if everyone’ll come together and we can figure out what’s what. I don’t know about you, Mike, but I don’t really want to stand around outside.“

“Shirley and I want everybody to come on over. She’s making coffee right now. I already asked the people I called, an’ called a few more. They’ll be here in about ten or fifteen minutes. Can you get the others plus any we missed? Then our neighborhood’ll be here.”

“I’ll call them right now,” said Michael. “See you in a few.”

The neighborhood stood and sat in the Zimmermans’ front room. A few sat on the carpet, leaning against a wall. Shirley found as many pillows as she could manage when she saw that folks were settling themselves on the floor.

Coffee was ready. She got out extra cups and put them on the kitchen table, along with a bowl of sugar and a small pitcher of cream. As folks came in the front door, Fred sent them to the kitchen first, to pour themselves a cup of coffee and to help themselves to the cookies Mrs. Yablonski brought. She had just finished baking when Michael called her and had quickly folded up a large towel with cooling cookies on her way out the door.

Fred said to Michael, "Everyone's here that I called. You?"

"Yes. I think so. I think everybody brought their kids."

Angela and the boys were with Joy, and other neighbors who had children had them in tow, stuffed bears and all.

"I don't think anybody wanted to leave someone alone. Good thing Mrs. Yablonski brought those cookies. The kids're busy for right now anyway."

Fred spoke out, " Hi, everyone. Thanks for coming."

He didn't know how to begin so just said, "When you all said that just like us, you thought strange things might be happening in the neighborhood, we thought we all oughta get together and figure out a plan. Anybody got any ideas?"

Mr. Owens said, "Yeah, I wanna know what's going on. I don't even know how to say what I'm wondering, but something's wrong."

People were nodding and agreeing and looking at each other. No one spoke up to say that they weren't worried.

Someone called out, "Maybe we should look around. See if there's anything around our houses. Check out back yards and behind garages."

Michael voiced what others hadn't said out loud yet. "What about the woods behind us?"

Mrs. Yablonski said, "It's dark now. It might not be safe. What about tomorrow?"

"I don't think we can wait," Fred spoke up. "Anyone been hearing scratching noises outside?"

"Yes." "Yeah." "For sure." "Yep, they're weird, and I don't like 'em." This last comment came from Mr. Owens. "Something's making 'em. It's pretty clear they aren't just imagination."

Joy, who had positioned the boys between Angela and herself, said, "Who do we know who lives on the other side of the woods? If we call them and they're ok, then we don't have to check those meadows, at least not right now."

Shirley said from the kitchen door, "We know the Frakes. They own that first farm, the one with that nice old barn and the Jersey cows in the front field. We go to the same church. It's social, and we do things like potlucks and have clean up days for some of the folks. We've gone to a few of 'em together."

Tom Smithfield, who lived on the other side of the Zimmermans, asked, " Do ya think they'll be ok about why we're asking what's going on?"

Shirley replied, "They're really nice people, and they'll be honest with us. I don't think they'll question what we're saying. I'll give them a call."

While folks continued to talk, she went over to the phone on a small table to the left, just inside the kitchen. She and Fred still had a landline they kept active, but like just about everyone else, they both had cell phones too. She picked up the receiver, but there was no dial tone. She clicked the receiver several times and checked the lines to the phone's base, but everything looked all right. Just no dial tone.

She put her head around the corner and said, "Phone isn't working. I'll go get another one."

A few folks looked up, and one asked, "Is it a landline?"

"Yes."

The room grew quiet except for a few restless children. People looked at one another. Meanwhile, Shirley went into the kitchen, retrieved another phone, and called the Frakes. People were beginning to murmur with each other again.

When she came back to the doorway, Shirley announced that the Frakes had taken her seriously and were concerned, but they hadn't seen or heard anything, and their animals were behaving normally. They had come in from feeding and the rest of the evening chores not too long before. There was nothing out of the ordinary over there.

"That's good," said Fred. "I guess we oughta look around the neighborhood."

Tom Smithfield voiced what everyone was thinking but was avoiding. "Well, we've gotta check the woods. At least we know it's ok further past 'em. Thanks for that, Shirley."

She nodded from the doorway. "Anyone want more coffee? There are more cookies here, too."

She picked up a plate of cookies and started them around the room. She sent some napkins with them. Then she picked up the coffee pot and started to re-fill cups. She ran out less than halfway around the room and headed back to the kitchen to make another pot.

She came to the doorway and said out loud, "I'm going to keep on making coffee. We have a couple of thermoses and a few other containers. I'll keep them on the kitchen counter near the creamer and sugar. Help yourselves whenever you want any."

Mrs. Yablonski said she'd bring over the rest of the cookies, and Harriet, Tom's wife, said they had things for sandwiches. She'd make some and bring them over. Joy offered to make some too. Someone offered to bring by some little snacks, and someone else offered a bundt cake.

They agreed to go in groups of three or four because it seemed safer that way. No one said anything about weapons, but a few folks had pocket knives, and one neighbor had a hunting knife with him. Nobody mentioned guns. Someone spoke out that they had to be careful for each other's safety and to think before acting. People were nervous enough already, he added.

A few women who didn't have children said they wanted to go with their husbands. One said she was taking a baseball bat, and another got up and headed to the door to stand near her husband and another couple to form one of the groups.

Those who had children started to talk about keeping them all together in one place with a few people, leaving more folks available to go out and help check. It seemed logical, and others agreed.

As the small groups formed, someone from one of them called out, "We're headed through everyone's back yards and the trails by the woods." Another yelled, "We're taking front and side yards." Someone else shouted as three people headed to a trail to the woods, "We're goin' to take the trail around the side of the block an' check the edge of the woods there an' look down the streets next to us."

Michael went with Fred and Tom. Tom called, "We're goin' into the woods. We're gonna follow the trails in there."

As they went out the front door, Fred said, "Hang on, I've got a real strong light in the garage. Lemme grab it."

He made a beeline for the side door to the garage and emerged only a minute later, holding a large, high beam, LED flashlight. It penetrated the growing darkness for a long way in front of them, and its light cut a broad swath.

Michael felt for the pocket knife in his jeans. He saw a tire iron leaning against the garage and picked it up as they went by. They headed to the back of the Zimmermans' house, past the yard, toward one of the several trails that led into and around the woods.

Other groups headed out, people went for more food, Shirley put on more coffee, and a few went with Joy to set up small sleeping bags, little tents, and toys in her front room for the kids.

Michael, Fred, and Tom kept their eyes peeled for any movement and listened for sound, but all they heard was the rustling and footsteps they were making as they followed the path between the two houses. It continued on and became a trail into the woods.

Tom said, "Maybe we need to try to be a little quieter. So we can see something instead of scare it away."

"What do you think we'll see?" asked Fred.

"I dunno. But it has to be something that can climb walls. Do ya think it might be in the trees?"

"No idea," said Michael, "But that's a good thought. It has to be something that can hang on and pull itself around. That's why I was thinking about raccoons."

Fred took a deep breath, and then in a low voice said, "Raccoons don't scare you or make you wonder what's outside that's so bad. They just pad along and mess things up."

"Well, let's go," said Tom, "And find out what it is. And get rid of it."

Michael didn't say anything but continued on with the other two. He couldn't say what he really felt, that this was different, that this was, well, hostile. That's what he had felt, a sense of evil. He knew the others felt it too, because he could see it on their faces and in their reactions. Fred was contemplating what was out there, and Tom was firming up his determination to fight it and be done with it. But somehow they all knew it was something more than a natural event.

He had noticed it in Fred's front room, too. Some folks looked a little cowed, some were shy, some spoke in an overly aggressive manner, but all were showing the outer edges of their discomfort and the fear they were beginning to feel. There was more to this than they wanted to voice. They didn't want to give credence to it.

The goal was to find out what was happening and what the players were. Not who, but what. Michael was aware that even though no one said that, they understood it.

Just before they actually entered the woods, they saw a small group with flashlights looking into corners of the back yard of a house two doors down. Two more people were headed across the street, where they used their flashlights to check outer walls and roofs. Another group had reached the next cross street, and flashlights were pointing up and down the street, around parked cars, and behind trees and shrubs to check the boundaries of their little neighborhood. They saw a few groups of children heading into Michael and Joy's house, guided there by a couple of adults.

The path on which Tom, Fred, and Michael were walking was becoming overgrown with foliage from trees and shrubs. They felt enveloped in darkness. Tom and Michael used their flashlights to illuminate the path in front of them, and Fred, with his high beam, lit up the canopy in broad arcs.

They grew quieter. They hadn't been speaking much, but when they did, they spoke in undertones and stepped softly along the path. They found themselves listening intently to whatever might be around them. Sounds of others searching around the neighborhood grew distant.

These woods were not especially deep, there weren't many thickets in them, and meadows and farms were not very far away on the other side, but they were still woods, not houses on streets with street lights. Something could lose itself in these woods.

As they continued to look around, past trees, up into

trees, and behind bushes, they imagined they heard faint scratching sounds. After they'd gone another fifty feet or so, it became clear that they weren't imagining it. The sounds were there, in front of them and off to their right. And not near the ground. The sounds came from the trees.

Tom asked very quietly, "Everybody hear that?"

"Oh, yeah," answered Fred.

"Me too," added Michael.

"What the bloody hell is it?" Tom's voice was puzzled, and there was an element of apprehension in it.

"I dunno. Let's find out," said Fred. He continued to search into the trees and the treetops. He became even more deliberate and methodical, covering a considerable area with his light. Tom aimed his flashlight at the edges of the areas Fred's light didn't cover, and Michael kept his flashlight going back and forth to light the path and immediate area where they were walking. They automatically became a cohesive unit and were moving more closely together now.

Michael whispered suddenly, "What's that? Up there, in that tree a little off to the right."

Fred aimed his light ahead, up, and to the right. Yes, something was moving in the tree. At first it looked like movement in the leaves and branches, but they heard the telltale scratching sound and saw that something was actually near the center of the tree. It seemed to be scuttling up about where the tree trunk would be.

They looked closely, but it was only a dark shape, and it

seemed to move in a jerky movement. Maybe that was because it appeared to be hunched over or hump-backed. They couldn't see very well because the shape was as dark as its surroundings. They saw movement only because Fred's bright light allowed it.

Whatever it was seemed to scurry upward. They could hear it now, even more than they could see it. It kept climbing, up into the darkness of the canopy. They lost sight of the movement, but they could still hear it, although the rustling and slight scraping noises were less audible, more muffled in the foliage.

Tom said, " Do ya suppose there's more of 'em? All of us heard those noises."

"I don't know how to put this," Michael said slowly, "But when you guys heard it before, did you have a funny sort of sensation?"

"I still have it," Fred spoke up. "I've been keepin' a close eye on the house and especially Shirley all evenin'. I don't know why."

"Feels like something's gonna go down, but you don't know what's comin'," said Tom.

"I felt nervous at first," said Michael. "Then I knew that I have to protect my family because there's a threat, like danger, like really bad karma."

"Like something evil." Fred finally stated it.

"Just like that," said Michael.

"I think so too. I just didn't say it out loud," said Tom. He looked at Fred, and then Michael. "Hey, I've never been good at admitting stuff like this."

"Well, we gotta figure out what it is. Or I guess it's what they are. I'm not sure how to get rid of something when we don't know what it is," said Fred.

"Do you suppose they're in the trees? It fits, because they were climbing our walls with claws or something that makes those noises. Wish I knew how many there are. Where do you suppose they came from?" Michael, like Fred and Tom, was looking around and up into the darkness while he spoke.

"It's almost like they just showed up. I never heard them before," said Fred.

"Well, they climb. Wonder if they dig or burrow or somethin' like that," offered Tom.

"Maybe we should walk a little further and see if we can spot another one," said Michael. "Maybe we can tell what it is."

Tom said, "Ya know, I don't know how you guys feel, but I really don't care what it is. I want to get rid of it. Or of them."

"It isn't natural to feel like we do, and like I think everyone else does too. We aren't safe," said Fred. "They're scarin' us. I wonder how we can scare *them*. You guys have any ideas?"

Michael said, "You guys think they left our neighborhood? I don't remember hearing any scratching at your house, Fred, but everyone was talking and kids were restless. You hear anything then?"

"I didn't," said Tom. "You, Fred?"

"Nope. Lemme check in with Al Owens. I gave him a two-way radio. I think Shirley said that she heard some others say they had cells and walkie talkies they were gonna get, so people could stay in touch when they were out checking."

"Al, Fred here. You find anything?"

A crackling voice came back, "No, no one's seen anything here."

"Heard anything from the others? Any outside noises like we all heard earlier?"

"We've heard from a few others, and all's quiet in the neighborhood. What's happening with you guys?"

Fred wasn't sure how much he wanted to say, but both Tom and Michael waved him on, urging him to tell Al about everything. So he did.

"Oh my Gawd!" exclaimed Al through the static and crackles. Then he added, "I won't scare anybody but I'll let 'em know that there's something in the trees in the woods."

"OK," said Fred. "Does anybody have any ideas why those things prob'ly left the neighborhood and came into the woods? If we can find out, maybe we can do something with it."

"Good thinkin'," came through the radio. "I'm gonna be all over it right now. I'm gonna stay in close touch with you guys too. You gotta be careful, ya hear?"

"Got it," said Fred. "We're watchin' out here. Any ideas, let us know so we can start something."

The three men looked at each other.

Then Michael said, "Maybe we should look around for more of 'em. There have to be more of 'em. We all heard 'em, and we all felt 'em too. One by itself couldn't have been everywhere at once."

They were uneasy, but they knew that was right. They had edged back in the direction of the neighborhood, not very far, but enough to be on a part of the path that was a little more open. They felt better there, even though no one acknowledged that.

"OK," said Tom. "You're right, we gotta know where they all are."

Fred added, "Maybe they're all in here," meaning the woods. "They climb, there are trees here, and it's dark. We felt 'em earlier in the evening, but we didn't hear 'em until we were inside and it was growing dark."

Michael said, "That's about when we heard them too. I think Angela knew something before that. She sensed it."

"We saw that," said Fred. "Both Shirley and I noticed it. She watched the boys real close. When she got up from the lawn, she was real quick about getting them inside. It was almost like she was running scared."

"She was," said Michael. "Joy and I saw it, but we didn't know why. Sometimes she has a sort of time out when she remembers her folks and all that happened. We just try to be there for her. I think we thought it was that, at least at first."

"Ya know," mused Tom, "If these things are all right around here, there's gotta be a reason. Wherever they came from, they got here somehow. I figure they can leave here, too. We just hafta figure out how."

"OK," said Fred. "We know they move up, not down. We couldn't really see what that one was. But I didn't think it was the usual sorta critter that you might see in here."

He continued, "If they go higher, do you suppose they might have something like bat wings to get 'em in the air?"

"Maybe they came in by air," said Michael. "It would explain how they showed up so suddenly."

"And how we felt, too," said Fred. "If something like that was hangin' out over your head, it'd feel horrible, like you were being pinned down. That's how Shirley and I felt. It's why we came out on the front porch, to shake it off."

"Didn't work, did it," stated Tom. "OK, we better look around."

Just then the two way radio crackled. Embedded within the static, Al's voice said, "Hey guys, everybody's sayin' they heard the scratching, an' it looks like they all heard it about the same time. Can't be exact, but that's the way it's looking."

Fred asked, "Did anybody notice anything different when we were goin' out to see what we could find? Anything we could use to keep 'em away from us?"

"Workin' on it, " replied Al's voice amid the crackling of the radio. "So far the only thing we can think of is that we all came out at the same time an' since then, no one's heard anything. 'Course, no one's been home, but no one's called any of us right here, either."

"We're gonna see if we can find more of 'em in here. It's dark in here, so maybe it's an idea to turn on as many outside lights in the neighborhood as we can find. Whaddya think?"

"We'll do it right now."

They heard voices in the background of static. "Got it!" "Doing it now." "I got flood lights I'll turn on." "Turning on whatever we got." And more voices further in the background.

Al's voice came through the radio again. "Some of us are gonna come and help you. We didn't see anything here, but you saw somethin' there. It's dark, and there're only three of you. Where're you at?"

"We came in on the path behind our house," said Fred. We're not very far in right now. Should take you only a few minutes to get here."

He added, "We wanna get goin' back in there because we figure there're more of 'em. Hurry!"

As he waited for a reply, they heard several people clumping and hurrying toward them, a ways away yet but coming fast. It sounded like people were nearly running. Fred didn't get a reply, because Al and several others came into view through the shrubbery.

"Let's go get 'em." Al called out.

They caught up to Tom, Fred, and Michael. Flashlights were set to high beams. A few were aiming what looked like hand held floodlights into the underbrush and through trees. Those lights lit up the whole area.

"The one we saw was in the trees," said Fred.

Michael said, "We didn't see much more than movement and a sort of hunched back. It kept moving up the tree trunk. Seemed like it was clawing its way up there."

They decided to look up into the trees and for movement anywhere. As they were talking about what else they could do and were heading further into the woods, they came to the conclusion that when they all got together at Fred's and then came outside, the scratching noises seemed to disappear.

Michael said, "Maybe being sorta secretive is how they stalk us."

It was the first time anyone had actually used the word "stalk".

Al said, "Stalk. Yeah, that's it all right. It felt like a threat."

Folks agreed, nodding and speaking up. "Felt heavy." "I felt I had to protect the wife and kids." "We stayed close even though we didn't talk about it to each other." And more.

Michael said, "I watched the boys. Sat upstairs on the floor just inside their door. Checked on them a few times and followed those sounds all along the hall. Joy checked too. We both were watching out for Angela, too. She was pretty upset."

"Yeah, Shirley and I saw that when she was outside with the kids," said Fred.

Others spoke about how they'd felt earlier in the evening.

"Lemme ask you guys," said Fred, "Does anybody feel that same kind of feeling now?"

"No," replied Bill, a neighbor who lived a few doors away.

His wife Jody, who had come with him, said, "Somehow I began to feel better at Fred's house. It's like we were taking charge."

"Yep," noted Tom. "I just really wanna get those things

outta our neighborhood now."

"Let's get going. Let's really check out these woods." Ed, another neighbor, began to walk with determination further into the woods, shining his bright hand held lamp in sweeping motions back and forth, and up and down.

People fanned out but stayed in a loosely formed group. Collectively, the various lights they had did a good job of covering the area of the woods, a good distance into them and also up into the trees.

Bill called out, "Hey, what's that? What moved up in that tree?"

"That's what we saw too!" exclaimed Tom. "There go two of 'em!"

Two dark shapes, hard to see separately in shadows even with the lights, were definitely there and were headed further up into a tree. They hung on as though they were using claws. They blended together, then apart, as they climbed. They were a little hunched, and then they seemed to blend into the darkness.

"They stopped I guess," said someone toward the back of the group. "Wonder why."

"That'll help us, I think," said Michael. "If we know where they need to be and we can get them away from that, maybe they'll leave the same way they came."

"That's just it," said Tom. "I can't figure out how they got here."

"Well," noted Fred, "If they like to be near the top of trees, and they move around in the dark, must be they feel safe there."

"Wonder if they'd go higher," Al spoke up.

"Why d'ya say that?" asked Fred.

"Well, if they don't go higher, but they stay about where we lost sight of 'em, and if they don't like the light…," he broke off. "Can we make it so they go higher up and then the sun comes up?"

"By gawd we can try," said Tom.

Jody said, "We're taking charge again. They don't like that. Does anyone feel that threat now, you know, the one we all felt earlier?"

People were murmuring. It appeared no one was aware of it. Some of the men were uncomfortable talking about it, even though they knew it wasn't imagination.

"Ok," said Bill. "I'm gonna say something but I'm not sure why or what it means. I really don't know what I mean. When we began to feel uneasy earlier, there were a few times something sort of hit me. I dunno, call it a premonition."

He stopped. The others were listening intently.

"Go on," urged Michael. "What was it?"

"Well," said Bill, hesitating a little, "I thought I felt something…. Well, I thought it felt mean. Evil. It intended evil. I don't know what I mean. But that's how it felt."

Fred patted him once on the shoulder and said, "You're not alone. I'm willing to bet we all felt something like that. Only, no one's said it out loud yet. But I figure that's why none of us are taking this lightly an' why we need to do something now. It can't wait."

"We felt it at our house," said Michael. "I know Angela felt it."

"Ok," said Bill, "What if we drive 'em up the trees and keep 'em up there? Make 'em be visible when it gets light. Then maybe we can see what we can do or maybe they'll leave. I don't know, but maybe it'll happen."

"Best thing is," said Fred, "They'll be away from us during the night."

"Yeah!" "Right." "Let's do it." "We gotta go for it." People were talking, in agreement.

Fred said, "We'll hafta go through the woods and be sure we've found 'em all, or as many as we can. They don't like lots of people, so we better go in a loose group. It'll probably take most of the night."

"Everybody agree with that, or does someone have another idea? Whatever works does it for me."

Tom said, "Let's get it done."

Jody offered to go to Shirley and Fred's, let everybody else know what was going on, and bring back coffee and sandwiches. She said she'd hurry. If they would please stay close to where they were, others coming to help could find them. The more people, the better. With more people they could safely spread out and find those things crawling up trees.

It was going to be a long night.

About a half hour later, several people including Jody

and Shirley returned with large, covered cups of coffee, bottles of water, and sandwiches. They said that others were making more and would bring them out in another couple of hours. They'd come to the edge of the woods at this area, so if groups would please call or filter back this way, there'd be more food.

One neighbor had called authorities, but they didn't take what was happening very seriously, since the neighbor had used the word "threat" but couldn't support it with an example. People had already brought up calling for help when they were at Fred's house, but because of the very nature of the evening, most folks had already figured that basically, they were on their own. They were right.

A few women, including Joy, were gathered in her home in the family room with the neighborhood kids, who were having fun jumping in and out of sleeping bags and on air mattresses. Mr. Abercrombie, who was very elderly, was comfortably situated in Michael's recliner with a soft blanket behind his shoulders in case he became chilled.

People were counting neighbors, making sure that no one was isolated, being certain to gather in anyone who was alone, and confirming that people were connected and communicating. A few more walkie talkies were brought out, charged cell phones were in pockets, and Fred and Al still had the two way radios.

There were enough people to break into two good-sized groups. There were numerous lights of various kinds and sizes among them all. If batteries ran low, more were available in houses and garages.

They set off, pointing lights into the woods at various heights, moving them slowly back and forth, and keeping eyes peeled for any movement. They were beginning to feel a sense of empowerment now that they had a plan.

In the back of many minds was the tremulous thought that if any of these things turned on them, what would they do? It was comforting to know that whatever these things were, they weren't very large. It was very comforting to know that these things seemed to run away from groups of people and didn't want to be around light. They proceeded with the vague plan they had.

After a couple of hours during which the two groups kept in contact, Al radioed Fred that their group, which had headed in a direction that they thought would give them fairly good coverage of the east side of the woods, was looking at three more of the creatures. In the background the group could be heard shouting and making noise.

"They've gone up the trees!" shouted Al gleefully.

"Hot dog!" chortled Tom.

At just that moment, Michael spotted something moving in the shadows ahead of them. It was at eye level, and it seemed to be moving forward, away from them. He pointed it out to the others. They were five altogether.

Then Tom cried out, "Look out, there's two more! Over there, to your left."

"Oh mannnn, three more further ahead, more to your right," came from Fred.

They began to yell, to holler, to stamp feet, and most of all to point lights where they saw movement. They flooded the area with the lights they had, and it seemed to work. Movements in the shadows kept ahead of them but seemed to be moving upward too.

The creatures were being driven. And no one stopped. Momentum encouraged them forward. They pressed on, using lights and noise to drive the creatures further and higher, toward the edges of the woods. When finally they could no longer see movement in any shadow even with illumination all around it, they stopped their activity.

While this was happening, they'd actively kept in contact with the other group to let them know what was going on and where they were. While they were driving this latest batch away from the neighborhood that they were reclaiming, others were chasing more creatures.

As the night wore on, groups searched, looked, shouted, and stamped feet along as many paths through the woods that they could find, paths that were near their neighborhood and led into the woods from it. Now and then a group came to a path's end, usually with a clearing or maybe a rock where folks could rest.

Even though these woods were not extensive, and the distance to meadows on the far side was perhaps a quarter of a mile as the crow flies, thickets and trees were fairly dense. No one wanted to be careless when searching through them.

The groups weren't especially methodical, but they were thorough, in the woods and in the neighborhood. People continued to keep in close touch with each other, with those who were with the children, and with those who were keeping watch within the neighborhood and at its edges.

Shirley and Ann, another neighbor, had assumed responsibility for finding and preparing food and drink for those who were out searching and were in close contact with people in those groups, and with everyone in the neighborhood. They quickly became the hub of updated information and delivered sandwiches, fruit, drinks, pop tarts, and any other quick snacks they had managed to find to folks in houses, folks patrolling the neighborhood, the two groups in the woods, and always staying together, checking back at a couple of clearings near the edge of the woods.

The night proved to be long and drawn out. Michael found himself marveling at how much people were able to keep themselves together and focused on the task at hand, although he knew logically that he shouldn't have been surprised because they'd all been threatened. Nevertheless it was heartwarming to see how neighbors had come together and were helping each other during this crisis. It said volumes for the neighborhood he called home.

Oh, sure, there were disagreements here and there, a few minor outbursts of temper, a few disagreements, but surprisingly, nothing too intense. They all had bigger game to hunt, and they all knew the stakes even if they couldn't define them.

This wasn't simply about clearing the area of something strange and unexpectedly frightening, something unknown and weird, something whose origins they didn't know or understand, and something that everybody knew was malevolent and would harm them, even though nobody had been able to succintly voice that. They knew that if they didn't take care of this right then and there, their lives as they knew them would change. Knowledge about what was happening was felt deep within them. They didn't know how they knew. They just knew.

By the same token, they didn't know how their lives would change if they failed with the task at hand. There was an intense urge to be thorough and specific, and to chase these things away. They didn't know what they were fighting, but for some reason they knew the fight was a matter of life and death. Of their bodies? They didn't know. Maybe of their souls, or both.

It was the blackest darkness just before dawn. Michael, Fred, Tom, and the others in their group came for the fourth time to the far side of the woods, each time on a different path. They felt they'd covered their territory pretty well. They used their lights on the trees and thickets surrounding them on three sides, while Fred contacted Al by radio and called Shirley, Tom called a few others who were in other groups, and Michael checked on Joy and everyone else at their home and nearby.

The other group was in sight of a small clearing on the neighborhood side of the woods. During the night, each group searching the woods had found itself on the far side near meadows at least twice.

Blackness began to give way to charcoal. Hand held lights still pierced the fading night with brilliant light that was beginning to lose its sharp contrast. Normally, woodland inhabitants would be awakening, some beginning to chirp softly, but the silence in the woods was palpable.

They were finally going to see their enemy. They still hovered in groups in safe places.

The sky was lighter grey now. Flashlights were almost superfluous, and there was a faint tinge of dusky rose toward the eastern horizon. People couldn't help themselves. They looked up, around, and into the trees.

Up toward the canopy were hunched, small, black shapes, appearing to cling closely together in small groups, just as the neighborhood had done through the night.

There was no feeling of fear or dread, but there was an intense caution due to an overall heaviness with more than a hint of malice. Sharply pointed heads with what appeared to be extended beaks and glittering eyes were watching people on the ground.

As the light grew, it became apparent that their hunched appearance was not because they were nervous or frightened. It was how they were built. They had what appeared to be large, folded arms at their sides, and they seemed to have short, stubby tails that didn't seem to be feathered but rather more reptilian.

However, it was their demeanor that was unnerving.

They stared maliciously down at the others, who were staring up at them. They didn't move except to watch the ground.

Then, as the sky became lighter, and orange and gold began to spread on the eastern horizon, the creatures became restless, almost fidgety. They looked around, and they looked at the sky. They shifted, and folks could see that they were standing on two thick legs that ended in what appeared to be claws. There seemed to be only two large claws per foot, but someone saw a much smaller third claw.

The creatures stretched out so they became taller, but they were still short. They continued to stare down with a baleful glare. When they looked toward the lighter part of the sky, now turning from warm tones to a faint blue, it was almost with disdain. Or perhaps their odd beaked heads gave that impression. No one thought of disdain. People simply understood that this was disdain, disrespect, and hostility in the same way they understood they were threatened.

The impression was of something that was disgusted. Disgusted with the new day that was dawning, with the beautiful kaleidoscope of colors that were changing and interweaving, creating new values and hues with every second. They felt like the creatures would turn it all grey, black, and bottomless if they could.

Then, the creatures stared intently at people on the ground again. If they had lips, the sensation was that those lips would be curled back in a snarl. They fidgeted more, some seemed to reposition themselves and stand up even a little taller, and some unfolded their arms, long, webbed extremities, and held them up and out at each side.

Now it was clear how they had arrived. They had flown into the neighborhood.

People were calling, radios and walkie talkies were squawking, people were pointing up at them and exclaiming, and more than a few were looking for cover. It wasn't clear to anybody that they wouldn't become targets.

And yet the feeling of disgust thrust upon them seemed to be fading away to a more raw impression of a haughty fury exuding from the creatures. No one understood how that happened, how people seemed to know what the creatures wanted them to feel, but therein lay much of the evil of it.

They had been threatened, and they had been afraid. Actually they had been terrified. It was only when they had been forced by fear and confusion to call each other that they had been able to regroup and plan, and only when they had all come together that their common need generated support from one to another, there for the offering and for the taking.

They still shared intense distrust of the unknown that was facing them, and they were still human with all the foibles and personality quirks that came with that. But they had learned powerful lessons during the last evening and night. The primal screams that were so close to happening began to fade just a little, but those still existed just barely out of reach of consciousness.

Evil might dissipate, but it wouldn't die and was cunning

about finding different ways to invade. Its polar opposite worked the best to keep it at bay. Generally, that involved caring, trust, kindness, compassion, concern, ways that made bad things good. Ways that brought about happiness, peace, and good will. Ways that were part and parcel of the infinite variations of expressions of love.

But everyone was still human. This night would not be forgotten, but its lessons might fade. Evil worked that way.

Michael, Fred, Tom, others in their group, the other group that had also searched the woods, people checking back yards, people caring for others, people preparing food, and people bringing food around, all looked upward. Cell phones, radios, and walkie talkies were and had been very busy, so everybody knew what was there and what had happened during the night. Most saw movement stirring, and all were able to feel fury from the creatures who were now exposed and near tree tops.

No one had a feeling of having won anything. They felt they needed to hang on until those things left their lives, but they didn't know how or when that would happen.

The sun rose over the horizon, and the sky was growing brighter by the minute.

The creatures at the tops of trees stretched out even more and began to extend their arms, or the things that looked like their arms. As those webbed appendages were extended, they appeared to be rather thick, broad, and leathery, and they seemed to be moving up and down. There was nothing graceful about the movement, but it seemed to be enough for creatures to be able to lift off the tree limbs where they had been, and slowly, slowly, with clumsy and erratic movement, head away to the south. People could hear flapping sounds, but otherwise the creatures were silent.

They rose singly or in two's or three's from several places in the woods, although all of them seemed to come out of those parts of the woods that were adjacent to the neighborhood that they had disrupted, where people had searched throughout the night. It took some time for a mass of them to be seen from the ground. The earlier ones seemed to move slowly, and later ones seemed to move in jerky, rather frantic flight to catch up with the others. They weren't flying very far above the ground, just skimming tree tops and roofs.

It looked like there were probably a couple of dozen of them in total. They still headed south. By the time they had grown smaller to the onlookers, they appeared to be in a mass, although not a solid one because they didn't fly well or in unison. But they flew. And it was away from the neighborhood.

Then an odd thing happened. As distance between the neighborhood and the flapping mass grew, although the mass wasn't that far away yet, the creatures began to shimmer. People strained their eyes not really accepting what they were seeing, but there were the creatures, shimmering in the sky, becoming less and less distinguishable *from* the sky.

A sort of transluscence happened in the place where everyone thought the mass was, and then it was gone. It didn't disappear in the distance. It simply disappeared from eyesight. And earshot.

After a moment or two, Michael said to anyone who was listening, “Does anybody feel anything?”

“Nope,” said Fred matter-of-factly. “Everything, the air, everything, feels like it did before all this.”

Tom let out a loud whoop. “They’re gone!”

He cheered, and they heard more cheers and happy yells coming from places in the neighborhood and from the edges of the woods. They could hear people running to each other, wives to husbands, husbands to wives, friends to other friends, kids out into yards.

“Didja *see* that?” “Hey man, we’re good now!” They’re *gone*! They’re outta here!” “Everyone ok?” “Everybody here?” People were talking and calling all on top of each other’s voices and were all over each other, waving, hugging, with high fives everywhere. The overall mood was jubilant, along with pieces of anger, puzzlement, concern, brief apprehension, and practical actions of making sure everybody, homes, yards, and neighborhood were secured and safe.

Michael met Joy in their front yard and pulled her, Angela, and the boys into a family bear hug. Friends and neighbors were milling about, happy to see anybody and everybody.

Shirley came out onto her and Fred’s front porch, put two fingers in her mouth, and managed a shrill, very loud whistle. Folks looked up at her, startled, but smiles were everywhere and were infectious.

"Pancakes're *on*!" she called out. "C'mon, there's bacon, scrambled eggs, lots'a syrups and jams, butter, the works!"

Those who had remained on patrol in the neighborhood all night had raided their pantries, and a few had begun to help Shirley as soon as it was light. They hadn't known yet what would happen, but they wanted to be sure everybody had a good breakfast. Now, it was a lively, exuberant breakfast celebration.

People filed in the Zimmermans' front door. Some stayed inside while others emerged with plates of food, napkins, silverware in hand, and fresh coffee in Styrofoam cups. After the meeting the night before and during the night, lawn chairs, benches, and more had migrated to the Zimmermans' front yard. People with full plates made themselves comfortable, and cheerful, animated conversations sprang up all over the yard.

Chairs and people spilled over into Michael and Joy's front yard too. A picnic table that was in a narrow side yard between the two homes was crowded with kids. Mothers and others including Angela and even old Mr. Abernathy were carrying smaller plates out to them, helping the younger ones with the hearty breakfast.

Fred wandered over to Michael, who was watching it all and feeling an immense sense of relief.

"Well," said Fred quietly, "Guess that's that."

Michael looked searchingly at him.

"For now," noted Fred. "What d'you think, Mike?"

In a low undertone, Michael said, “I don’t know what I think. Too many questions with no answers. Doesn’t have to be all buttoned up, but …. This was serious, Fred.”

He went on. “Why don’t we know more? How do we know what to do about this? No one’s gonna believe us.”

Fred contemplated, then spoke, “Nope, I think you’re right. Even with all the photos people were taking with their phones, my gut tells me we’re still gonna be on the outside about this one.”

He went on, “ Do ya think that those things left because they were afraid of us?”

“No way,” said Michael. “ I think we got really lucky this time. They don’t like lights…..” his voice trailed off, because he didn’t know exactly what it was he wanted to say.

“But they might come back,” said Fred. “Yeah, I think so too.”

“Any idea why they came, what they are, and all the rest of it?”

“No. Haven’t come up with anything. At least we can recognize what it’s like when they’re here. And they were really sorta easy to chase away.”

“How long d’you think we should let everybody relax before we ask a few others about it and then get everyone together again? At least we could figure out a communication system of some kind so we’re not caught off guard,” said Michael.

“Good idea,” agreed Fred. He mused, “I wish I knew what they wanted. You felt like they were stealing your life away.”

"Maybe that's part of what they wanted, or maybe that's how they go about getting whatever it is they're after. It's like they live in the darker areas of life – hell, of *us*. We all felt it. Maybe they feed off it."

"I don't know," said Fred quietly. "I don't know how to analyze something like this."

Just then, Shirley came over to her husband with a platter of more pancakes and bacon, looked at them both, and then said, "OK, out with it."

"Out with what?" asked her husband.

"You don't know what to do with this, do you? Well, we talked about that during the night around here. We don't have answers, and we feel, well, a little smaller because of it all."

"Any solutions?" asked Michael.

"No," replied Shirley. "But what we did all together worked for us. Have to trust that," she said. "Have to keep it going, too."

She put more pancakes and bacon on their plates and headed off to other folks with empty plates.

They knew it wouldn't be easy because it wasn't as familiar as old habits were, but they also knew that it had to be. They had to continue on. Their neighborhood hadn't been especially close before, and the immediate threat was gone, but at that moment they felt as though they were in a good place to begin to establish thoughtful habits and customs built on supportive foundations.

They appreciated that with a little courage and cooperation, they had managed for now to look after their neighborhood. They just wanted to live their lives, and they wanted their children to be able to do the same. The future mattered.

Index

About the Author

The author's formal education is in cultural anthropology, wildlife biology, and ethnomusicology. This seems to naturally lead to an ecosystemic approach in lots of directions.

www.ingramcontent.com/pod-product-compliance
Lightning Source LLC
Chambersburg PA
CBHW060117260626
47160CB00005B/1919
* 9 7 8 0 9 8 5 5 1 0 9 8 5 *